Breaching the Parallel
The Future Past, Book 1
by MW Anderson

This is a work of fiction. Names, characters, organizations, places, events, and incidents are either products of the author's imagination or are used fictitiously. Any resemblance to actual persons, living or dead, or actual events is purely coincidental.

Copyright © 2017 by Mark Anderson
All Rights Reserved.

No part of this publication may be reproduced, distributed, or transmitted in any form or by any means, including photocopying, recording, or other electronic or mechanical methods, without the prior written permission of the publisher, except in the case of brief quotations embodied in critical reviews and certain other noncommercial uses permitted by copyright law.

Special Thanks to

Amanda Anderson, for supporting and encouraging my writing and proof reading drafts.

Craig Boehman, dependable proof reader and a creative sounding board during my early years. He is a remarkably creative person.

Master Sergeant Scott F. Sullivan, a Cavalry Scout during the last years of the cold war. He has been my chief military adviser for 30 years and a valuable proof reader. Thank you for your service in dangerous places.

Scott Kahler, for helping me turn my concept and 8-bit art into a dramatic book cover and also for proof reading the first draft.

Other proof readers that gave feedback:
Charles and Jan Anderson (aka Dad and Mom), Ray Anderson,
Henry Black, Kris Sarratt, Steve Rowe, Jim Evermon
and Aaron Mast.

Chapter 1: The First Parallel

Looking out the window of his command vehicle, Colonel William Erickson could see a column of tanks stretched out in the dark before him. The group was moving hastily across the North Korean countryside. He could only see a few of them in the clear but moonless night, but he knew they were there, vehicles of the 4th Armored Cavalry Regiment, *his* regiment.

Returning to his work station at the rear of the vehicle's conference room sized cabin he put his headset on just in time to hear a woman's voice say, "Colonel, the anti-aircraft section says they have a visual on the enemy helicopter, it just cleared the ridgeline ahead."

"Tell them to engage," he replied.

A moment later the colonel noticed a brief flash from a side window and held his breath until three seconds later a brighter flash appeared out the front window.

"Send my thanks to the reconnaissance aircraft for the early warning," he instructed.

"Colonel," came the gravelly voice of the man seated next to him, "so far, no other resistance ahead and no reports of trouble on either flank."

"Thank you Major."

Erickson looked to his monitor which showed the location of all of his unit's vehicles, based on their GPS data, overlaid on a topographical map of North Korea. Looking at the display was not unlike watching a video game unfold before him. This gave the colonel a level of information and situational awareness that was mere fantasy back in 1950 during the *First* Korean War. But was a welcome addition now that the Second Korean War had begun in earnest.

The colonel still couldn't believe things had turned out this way. Tensions with North Korea had risen steadily over the previous year culminating in the deployment of most of the US Army's powerful I Corps near the border the month before. But even with this deterrent in place the North *still* launched an invasion of South Korea. Erickson reasoned that the North's leadership had to know that it was a hopeless fight, unless reaping wanton destruction on Seoul, which sadly they accomplished, was their only spiteful goal.

The plan for victory against the North was similar to that first war. An amphibious invasion by Marines on the western coast and armored thrusts at several locations by the Army across the 38th parallel of latitude, roughly the border between North and South Korea.

Colonel Erickson switched his display to a larger scale map that showed the projected route of advance for his regiment. It went up the country's central mountainous region exploiting a series of valleys.

Major Baker leaned over, "You think we'll be able to get far enough without being detected to flank their reserves?"

Erickson replied without looking, "Yes major, I believe we will. As long as the air force keeps up the jamming and we deal with any ground forces encountered *quickly*."

The voice of the communications sergeant came over his headset, "Colonel, I Corps is on the radio for you."

"Connect me," Erickson replied.

A moment later he heard a click and said, "General?"

"Erickson, General Cornell here."

"I read you General, go ahead sir."

"Colonel, a tank company in our lead brigade combat team has run into a really nasty tank trap. It was well concealed and five tanks have been immobilized," the general said irritation in his voice.

Colonel Erickson thought about this for a moment, "Any word on how to spot it?"

"You know as much as I do Colonel, once I get a straight answer from the local commander, I'll get back to you. Until then, make sure you take appropriate measures. Cornell out."

Erickson switched back to his tactical display and decided that his forward elements were too bunched up.

"Major, General Cornell says we had tanks run into a well concealed trap. Let's get E troop to double their unit depth, and have the lead element get into a line ahead formation."

Major Baker nodded emphatically, "Yes sir, I'll get them squared away."

Colonel Erickson checked the time. Another hour and it would be time to top off fuel.

Hopefully things will stay quiet until after that.

Chapter 2: The Lieutenant

Lieutenant Pontus' 1st Scout Platoon of six M3 Bradley vehicles were leading the way for the rest of the 4th ACR and making fast time. Some old roads aided the advance and so did the recent dry weather, the ground was firm. The 30 ton vehicles' treads dug into and ripped up the turf where it was soft, but were not slowed significantly.

The lieutenant considered it fortunate that the unit had encountered almost no resistance so far, though they did have to skirt wide of two villages that were dark and quiet. They were dark because bombers had been taking out power stations since offensive operations had begun two days before and quiet because these people just didn't want to be bothered and curiosity was highly discouraged in this country.

Still, John Pontus was anxious. He was proud that his platoon got to lead the way, but it was a big responsibility and he had never seen combat before. His training was thorough, and he had talked with many veterans who had described their initial experiences. Everyone told it a little differently and John expected that his first encounter would also be unique.

His Bradleys had just entered into a large valley. It felt good to get past the narrow entrance which was a natural choke point for the advancing armored vehicles. Now with more room to run, the risk to his vehicles and crews was reduced.

Pontus' mind wandered back a few weeks to the good byes he had exchanged with friends, family and most of all with his girlfriend Kathryn. He recalled how her teary eyes had fixed onto him…

"Contact!" yelled Sergeant Turner, his gunner.

Lieutenant Pontus snapped back to the moment and looked forward.

"Two B-M-Pees, their engines are hot but they're not moving," Sergeant Turner stated, "one thousand meters ahead, under some trees."

"Engage with cannon, armor-piercing," Pontus ordered sharply, but what he thought was, *smoke 'em*.

He repeated the order to the other vehicle commanders in his platoon via headset.

Lt. Pontus prepared to report the contact to his commander when the staccato bark of the Bradley's 25mm cannon interrupted him. He heard more cannon fire from outside the vehicle.

"Both vehicles hit," Turner said calmly.

The lieutenant was again about to report in when he heard and felt a tremendous explosion.

"What the hell was that!?" he said as he looked out his vision port.

The sergeant's voice raised in pitch as he replied, "Sir, there was a huge secondary explosion at the location of the B-M-Pees. It made a fireball one hundred feet in the air, far in excess of them just cooking off their onboard fuel and ammunition."

Focusing himself he reported the contact to Captain Pearce, his immediate superior. The captain told Pontus "good job" and ordered him to proceed. He would have another platoon investigate the remains of the BMPs.

Pontus' first contact with the enemy was over almost as soon as it had begun.

Chapter 3: The Reporter

Renee Carlisle was hanging on for dear life. It's not that she was delicate, she had ridden horses throughout her childhood. But bouncing around in the back of this tank, *Bradley* she reminded herself, was something else entirely. She was thankful for the helmet she was wearing as she'd banged her head a couple of times already.

"You okay ma'am?" the woman seated next to her asked.

"Yeah Sal, I'm doing okay," she lied, "and please call me Renee."

Another big jounce and Renee thought, *this thing belongs in a rodeo.*

"How long have you been at L-C-N?" Sergeant Sally Walker asked.

"Less than a year. Before that I was at N-B-C for four."

Sal chuckled, "A lot of the guys call it 'Left Coast News'."

Renee grimaced, she had heard that sardonic title many times.

"Do you have family out there, is that why you moved?" Sal asked.

Renee thought back to when she had first been approached by a producer from the Los Angeles Communication Network, LCN. At the time she had been languishing at NBC, where it had become a numbers game. Ratings were down and the number of people ahead of her was high.

"Well, my mom is in Montana, that's where I grew up, and dad is in Denver now. But I made the switch for the opportunity, to get more onscreen time," she said. "That and I decided that my last winter in New York was going to be my *last* winter there."

"Montana? We're neighbors then, I'm from Idaho," Sal flashed a genuine smile.

Renee looked over at Sal. She was tall, about the same height as Renee's five foot nine, but with a stockier frame. While Renee had played intermural volleyball in college, Sal looked like she might have played safety for her high school football team.

Since Renee's arrival at this posting as an embedded reporter Sal had been assigned to stay attached to her hip. She was a combination of babysitter and bodyguard, and Renee was glad on both counts.

"Montana seems like another reality to me now after almost ten years in New York," Renee said. "I prefer fast nights in the city to quiet evenings on the farm."

Boom

Renee felt a streak of fear run the full length of her body.

"What was that!?" she blurted out.

Lieutenant Norman's voice came over her headset, "One of the forward units engaged some enemy vehicles and there's been an explosion, but we're well away from it."

She knew he was trying to reassure her, which she didn't mind. It was bad enough being in this dangerous and unfamiliar environment, but she couldn't see a damn thing from inside the back of this tank, *Bradley* she reminded herself again. She didn't completely understand the difference between a tank and the vehicle in which she now sat. But she did know that as long as she just called them by their names, *the bigger one is an Abrams, the smaller one is a Bradley*, she wouldn't embarrass herself.

Norman's voice again, "My platoon has been tasked with investigating the area of the explosion. I'm sending three of my Bradleys to take a look, but we'll keep moving forward."

"Thank you lieutenant," she responded pleasantly.

The lieutenant tended to talk down to her. Not that he was arrogant, but rather like he assumed she didn't know anything about the army, which wasn't far from the truth. Like most men she encountered he was a touch flirty. He was always pleasant and proper in his conduct towards her but overall he seemed disingenuous. Most people wouldn't notice, but when it came to spotting a phony, Renee was a pro.

"Don't worry Ms. Carlisle, we should be pretty safe here," Sal said.

"Thanks Sal, but please call me Renee," she implored.

"Yes ma'am, I'll try," she responded.

Unlike Lieutenant Norman, the sergeant was down to earth and talked to her as a friend would. Renee liked Sal and appreciated her help. She just hoped that *Sal* wasn't good at spotting a phony.

Chapter 4: The Draftee

Private First Class Matt Murphy sat in the back of a different Bradley scout vehicle. He was looking at the tubes of TOW missile reloads mounted on the bulkhead opposite him when he heard his buddy's voice.

"Murph, I think we'll get some action tonight."

Murphy turned to Specialist Dominic Jones.

"What makes you say that?" he asked.

"That's my opinion as a professional soldier," Jones said, his southern accent distinct as ever. "After you see some combat, you'll know these things too."

Jones was regular army, not like Murphy the draftee. But he knew Jones hadn't seen any combat either.

"I can't believe you got drafted in the very first round," Jones screwed up his face. "Hey man, did ya get a million dollar signing bonus?" he laughed.

It wasn't the first time Jones had used this line on Matt. "No, but with my one year active service bonus I did buy a Jeep. Made my return to civilian life a lot of fun," he said, trying to gain the upper hand in the verbal sparring.

Jones' dark face frowned. Matt knew it bothered the regular army guys that after the required one year of active duty draftees got a $10,000 tax free bonus. But it had been necessary to cushion the political impact of the first draft in more than 40 years.

Jones' toothy smile returned, "Yeah, but you earning that Jeep now aren't ya? You thought your army career was over and now your ass is in the back of this can just like me."

Murphy looked up as he heard a distant explosion.

"See? What I tell you," Jones said.

Within a minute Murphy heard the vehicle commander speak over his headset. "First platoon took out a couple of B-M-Pees. We're going to dismount and have a look."

A few minutes later the vehicle came to a stop, Jones swung the rear door out and Murphy followed him out of the Bradley, M4 carbine in hand.

Murphy saw two other M3 cavalry scout vehicles come to a stop nearby and four other troopers ran out to meet up with he and Jones.

As a group they approached the site with caution being careful not to step on any debris, some of which was still burning. When they got closer Murphy saw that the two BMPs were still largely intact but had been flipped over, apparently by the force of an explosion.

"Jones, Murphy, check out those B-M-Pees, we'll investigate the explosion site," Sergeant Smith ordered, his facial features almost indiscernible in the night.

Matt ran along with Jones towards the BMPs, some 20 meters away. As they got near they slowed and approached cautiously. They weren't burning, at least that Matt could see, and they didn't hear the sound of ammunition detonating, 'cooking off,' inside.

Matt watched as Jones went up to the first BMP, which was lying upside down. The side hatch was sprung open part way and Jones put the muzzle of his assault rifle into it, nudging it open further. Peering into the darkness, he switched on a tactical light clamped to the side of his weapon. After a few seconds he ducked back out.

"Empty, no bodies, no equipment for a squad. Weird."

While Jones went to search the second BMP, Murphy scanned the surrounding area. He spotted something a short distance away. He approached and saw an object that was about ten feet by ten feet square but only a few inches thick. It looked like the roof of a shed. Another of the large squares was lying nearby.

Murphy returned to where Jones was and told him about the large squares.

Jones said, "Not sure what that would be for." Then pointing to the dead BMPs he said, "The second one's a zero too. Let's get back to sarge."

Murphy and Jones ran back to reunite with the other four of their party. They were walking away from a large hole in the ground.

"Hot as hell over there," the sergeant said with a grimace. "Smells like explosives and fuel of some kind. There's some open barrels in the bottom of the pit." He paused for a moment, looked around at the men and said, "Let's mount up, not much else to see here."

As they made their way back, Murphy told the sergeant about the square object he had seen. He took it in with a "huh."

"I'll relay it Private."

The men boarded their respective Bradleys and the three vehicles moved off in tandem, racing to catch up with the rest of their platoon.

Chapter 5: The Flash

"Colonel, UAV alpha-zero-two has detected a small thermal signature not far ahead, barely above ground heat level. It's small and faint, but definitely there," Specialist White said in her calm voice. After General Cornell's warning about concealed tank traps, and the surprise contact with the two BMPs just minutes earlier, Colonel Erickson had told the operators to look for even the smallest variation in heat.

Erickson moved to where he could see the thermal image for himself.

There it was, smack dab in the middle of the valley. He couldn't make it out clearly, but could see that it was small, only a few meters across at most, and had a regular round shape... something man made.

"Major, have the choppers take a look," the Colonel ordered.

A minute later, the colonel heard two helicopters fly over. He watched the live, night vision enhanced, images being taken from the choppers. The video zoomed in on a structure of some kind, very low to the ground, heavily draped with camouflaged netting.

"Have all units halt advance," the Colonel ordered. "Let's figure out what this is."

He felt his own vehicle come to a stop and, returning to his station, watched the situational map to ensure that the rest of the vehicles complied with the order.

FLASH

Colonel Erickson was blinded by a flash so intense that even the partially shuttered windows of the command vehicle didn't reduce its effect. Then in the next instant, there was only blackness.

He waited for his eyes to recover from the flash and after a few moments realized that he *could* see, but none of the monitors or instruments inside the command vehicle were illuminated. It was almost completely dark, like being inside a bank vault or worse... a tomb.

Then a light, someone was sweeping a flashlight around the compartment.

"Colonel, are you alright?"

Erickson recognized the voice of Corporal McCall his driver.

"Yes, I'm fine. What happened?" he countered.

"Don't know sir."

As the Colonel's mind started to race with the possibilities he heard the sound of a distant crunch, and then another. As his mind processed the sounds, the darkness was interrupted by a fireball some distance away, and then a second later the boom of an explosion resounded through the hull.

He saw Major Baker open the side door and lean outside, binoculars in hand. Inside, more flashlights were on now. Erickson moved to the front of the compartment, next to the driver who was fiddling with various switches. The major popped his head back in.

"It's the choppers sir, at least one of them went in hard and is ablaze, I can't see the other," he reported.

That pointed Colonel Erickson in a specific direction as to what happened.

"Get in touch with I Corps, tell them we may have been hit with an E-M-P," he said with anger. An electromagnetic pulse bomb had the ability to destroy electronic equipment over a large area from a long distance away.

Sergeant Gonzales replied, "So far my radios are dead, no power."

The Colonel was losing patience with the situation, but tried to suppress it. Just then, he heard the vehicle's engine turn over and the lights came back on.

Gonzales said, "Radios are back up sir, I'll try to raise Corps."

McCall, the young driver, looked at the colonel and said, "I just turned everything off and restarted sir, fired right up."

Erickson smiled slightly as he replied, "Very good Corporal." He felt a little foolish for his rush to judgment about an EMP, but something unusual had happened. And even with the engine off, the batteries should have given them some internal lighting.

"Let's head over toward the crashed chopper. Get our firefighting equipment out there a-sap," he barked to no one in particular.

Erickson heard the 600 horsepower diesel engine rev but the command vehicle just shuddered.

Corporal McCall, said, "ah damn, we might have thrown a track, or got stuck on something. I'll go take a look sir."

Erickson nodded and then headed back to Sergeant Gonzales to see if he could speak to the Corp Commander. As he arrived at the sergeant's station the man looked up at him, confusion plain on his face.

"Sir, so far I haven't been able to reach Corps or any of our squadrons," he said tentatively.

Colonel Erickson noticed the driver come back inside.

"Sir... we're stuck in the ground sir," he said matter-of-factly, shaking his head.

The colonel winced as he tried to understand, "Stuck? You mean mud? But this valley is dry as a bone. Did we hit a bog or a pond?"

Then the colonel thought, *tank trap...*

The driver looked a bit uneasy as he replied, "No, no mud sir. You should probably come take a look."

Colonel Erickson moved forward and called back to Sergeant Gonzales "Let me know the second you raise Corps."

Erickson stepped out of the vehicle and felt the ground firm beneath his boots, definitely not muddy. He looked around briefly

17

and saw several other vehicles from his Regimental Headquarters. A few had engines running, but none were moving.

He turned to look at the driver who was standing beside the large C2V command vehicle. Then noticed the barrel chested Major Baker kneeling, looking at the road wheels.

"This is pretty damn strange," the major said.

He looked up at Colonel Erickson then pointed his flashlight at the road wheels, which sit on top of the vehicle's metal tracks.

Erickson knelt down and then realized he couldn't see the tracks and that the road wheels were sunk into the ground at least 18 inches, maybe more. And they weren't just sunk in a rut, there was dirt in and around the road wheels, firm dry dirt with wild grass growing out of it. The grass wasn't bent over at all, it was sticking straight up in the large gaps between the road wheels, as if it had grown there while the vehicle sat.

Erickson stood back up and considered this, then realized he had no answer to the puzzle. He looked around at the other nearby vehicles. He could tell they were all sitting lower to the ground than they should be.

About ten meters away a Humvee was rocking forward and back and then climbed up out of the four holes its tires had been in. The colonel motioned for the driver to come over.

"Hold tight," the colonel said to the driver. Then stepping back up into the command vehicle he called out, "Gonzales, what have you got?"

Gonzales responded, "Still nothing from Corps, but I did raise E Troop. Captain Pearce says that his whole troop is immobilized with the exception of two M-threes."

"Tell Captain Pearce to send one of his mobile Bradleys to check out the chopper crash site. Also tell him and any other troop or company commanders you can reach to have their men dismount and setup a perimeter outward of our position," the colonel ordered. "Then have them start digging the vehicles out one by one."

Erickson stepped back down and approached the waiting Humvee. "I want you to head back to I Corps and let them know our situation, that the whole squadron is immobilized at the moment and it'll be hours before we are ready to resume our advance. Let them know we can't reach them via radio and ask if they have any orders for us."

The driver called out, "Yes sir!"

With that the colonel slapped the hood of the Humvee and walked away.

The pickup truck sized vehicle accelerated, turned around and sped towards the rear of the formation.

Erickson watched it go, hands on hips, and considered what to do next.

It was then that he noticed the glow of the bright, full moon overhead.

Chapter 6: First Responders

Lieutenant Pontus held onto the back of the turret of a Bradley as it moved deliberately toward the scene of the first helicopter crash. The second chopper was an inferno about 200 meters away, he could feel the intense heat even at this distance and they didn't have anything to fight such a blaze only hand held extinguishers. There was nothing they could do to help that crew should any of them have survived the landing. But as they got closer to the other wreck he thought it didn't look too bad. He was hopeful there would be survivors.

Dismounting the Bradley he saw now that the small aircraft had pretty much landed on its skids, either by luck or pilot skill. He realized as he thought about it now, the same thing must have happened to the helicopters that had happened to the tanks and Bradleys, their engines had shut down.

Approaching the pilot's side door with flashlight in hand Pontus saw movement. His heart raced as he pulled on the handle. It resisted him for an instant then gave way. The pilot raised one hand and John looked him over. He couldn't see any obvious signs of injury. He noticed now that the opposite side of the front windshield was badly smashed and the co-pilot wasn't moving.

Weakly, the pilot said, "my leg... ah, can't move it."

Lieutenant Pontus motioned one of his men over and together they slid the pilot out.

Pontus went back inside the cockpit and reached over to check on the copilot. He looked to be pinched inside the wreckage, getting him out wasn't going to be easy.

"Can you hear me?" he asked.

Pontus reached to feel the man's face and felt warm liquid. He switched to his neck to check for a pulse but couldn't feel one.

Exiting the vehicle Pontus helped carry the pilot back to the Bradley. As they moved he could see that the pilot was favoring his right leg, trying to keep it off the ground. They carefully maneuvered him through the back hatch of the Bradley and set him down.

"Is it broken?" the lieutenant asked.

The pilot replied through a grimace, "Yeah, I think so."

Pontus called out "Okay men, let's mount up and go find a medic."

The lieutenant and the other men got back into the armored vehicle and headed rearward to find the headquarters troop.

* * *

Colonel Erickson sat in his command vehicle thinking about the last few hours trying to come to terms with all the data he had in hand. Dawn had come but the mysteries were only deepening.

The Humvee driver he had sent to find the corps command had returned with frightening news. He hadn't been able to find any elements of the corps, or even the rest of their own regiment. What's more, his progress had been slowed by overgrowth of vegetation going back the way they had come just a few hours before. There had been no sign of the freshly tilled ground created by the tanks and other heavy vehicles of the regiment.

A technician approached and said, "Sir, I've investigated the GPS equipment in the command vehicle and of other nearby units. They all appear to be functioning, but for some reason they can't establish a link with the satellite network. They just report an error code and keep 'searching'."

The colonel considered this news. *Maybe an EMP in space could have knocked out the satellites and disrupted our systems, but where the hell is the rest of the regiment?*

"Alright, thank you," Erickson said.

"Colonel, I've got more news for you," came Sergeant Gonzales' voice.

"Go ahead," Erickson replied as he walked to the sergeant's station.

Gonzales began, "I've spoken with radio operators throughout the squadron, and also the signals intelligence guys and the situation is pretty easy to summarize. There aren't any signals out there besides ours. Not just on the command network, but we're talking no civilian radio traffic, no radio signals," he paused. "We aren't detecting the jamming from the Air Force, no radar signals from military or civilian sources. *Nothing...* sir," frustration clear in his voice.

Major Baker piped in, agitation apparent, "How could that be? You can't tell me that corps, the Air Force, hell even civilian radio are all gone? It has to be a mistake, the equipment must have been damaged by some kind of electronic warfare," he said.

Erickson saw what looked like desperation on the major's face.

"We can talk to each other, the units here in our group, just fine," the colonel said. "The equipment appears to be functioning."

It was becoming clear to Colonel Erickson that whatever was happening was beyond the bounds of weapons of warfare. There was a broader more unique problem that they needed to come to terms with.

"Major, the meeting is in fifteen, in my tent," the colonel said. "We'll start tackling these issues one by one. For now can you check on the rest of the headquarters vehicles and see how many are left to dig out?"

"Yes sir," Major Baker said and turned slowly to leave.

Erickson returned to his station and reviewed his notes for the meeting. The first page was a compiled list of the most recent muster of the unit.

4th ACR
- Regimental HQ and HQ Troop
    2 M3A3 Bradley
    8 of 12 M4 C2V Command vehicles accounted for
    AA section, 2 of 4 Linebackers present

- 2nd Cavalry Squadron
    HQ and HQ Troop
        2 M3A3 Bradley
        2 of 6 M4 Command vehicles
        2 M1135 NBC recon vehicles
    Eagle Troop (all accounted for)
        HQ Section
            1 M3A3 Bradley
            1 M1A2 Abrams
        1st and 3rd Scout platoons
            12 M3A3 Bradley
        2nd and 4th Tank platoons
            8 M1A2 Abrams
        Mortar Section
            2 M1129 MCV-B
    Fox Troop
        Only 3 M3A3 Bradleys present
    Grizzly Troop
        No vehicles mustered
    Husky Company
        11 of 14 M1A2 tanks
    Artillery Battery
        No vehicles mustered

```
- Support Squadron (muster incomplete)
     Supply Troop
          Heavy Trucks HEMTT
               2 M977 cargo
               5 M978 tankers
                    2 water
                    1 JP-8
                    2 Diesel

- Other (still counting)
     20+ trucks
     20+ hummers

- Personnel, approximately 500 (still
counting)
```

    It was only a fraction of what was in the table of organization and equipment he had reviewed for his regiment prior to the invasion.

    Erickson climbed down out of the tall vehicle, out into the bright sun. Nearby he saw one Bradley pulling another Bradley out of its hole with a tow cable.

    The colonel walked by the two long ruts where the vehicle had been stuck and peered down into them.

    "Huh," he said to himself and made a note.

    - *Grass*

Chapter 7: Theories

Inside his office, a large portable shelter, Colonel Erickson sat at a small table with his five most senior officers discussing the events of the previous night.

The Colonel said, "Based on what you've told me about two-thirds of our vehicles have been dug out so far. That's good progress. As platoon sized units get freed keep moving them forward and out to the edges of the valley. I don't want them in this area we got stuck in."

Erickson estimated that the parking situation would be handled within a few hours. After that they would focus on supplies.

"Sir, let's put the Linebacker anti-aircraft Bradleys up on the bare ridge just north of the valley," Major Baker said.

"Sounds good, do it," Erickson replied. "As the platoons get into position have them shut down, we have no significant quantity of reserve fuel."

"As I'm sure you all know. The communication and signals situation hasn't changed; we haven't been able to talk to anyone outside of this valley," he said. "As to the flash event itself, I haven't heard anyone with a contrary account." He saw heads shake.

Dr. Stone spoke, "The helicopter pilot said that he experienced the same thing the rest of us did, a bright flash and then all of his power was cut. He has two broken legs, but is otherwise in good condition."

This was the first time that Dr. Stone had made a comment at the meeting. Colonel Erickson wanted Major Stone to be present not just because he was a senior officer, but because he was one of the most intelligent people Erickson had ever known.

"Okay, that about does it for our tactical situation. Now let's talk about the unexplained and the just plain weird," the colonel

25

said bluntly. "Our vehicles were all stuck, planted in the ground, in an instant. How?"

The other men looked around at each other.

The colonel continued, "Don't be scared to throw out crazy ideas, it won't phase me, not today. General Cornell warned me that several tanks in another unit got stuck in a tank trap. Could what happened to us be the result of some kind of technology or technique meant to immobilize our vehicles?"

Lieutenant Colonel Brower, second in command to Colonel Erickson, offered, "An experimental device or weapon. Something supplied by either China or Russia to test out on us."

"An interesting idea, it would explain that condition we were in, but not where everyone else is. What else?" the colonel looked around.

Captain Pearce said, "As my men were digging vehicles out they noticed something else peculiar. The right rear corner of one of the Bradleys was missing. I went and had a look myself. It was a section a few inches deep and from top to bottom it was missing as if it had been cut off. The surface of what was left had a bumpy porous texture, a little like a cheese grater."

"Interesting," Erickson said. "On the way over here I noticed something else no one has mentioned. Down in the ruts where they pulled one of the Bradleys out, I saw that at the bottom was grass, green and healthy, although flattened, two feet down."

Captain James' eyes widened at this, "Yes sir, we noticed the same thing. Big wide swaths of flattened grass."

"Something else Colonel," the captain continued. "I'm sorry if this is the first you're hearing it. One of the tanks from my 2nd Platoon was in worse shape than just being sunk into the ground. It was actually half buried in the side of a hill."

The colonel leaned forward concerned, "The crew?"

"Fine, they were a bit scared, you see they weren't just in the side of a hill, the hill was kind of going right through the tank," the captain said. "There was grass, dirt, bugs, rocks all inside the hull, surrounding some of the men up to their chests. The driver was in the worst shape, but was able to open his hatch and breathe until he could be dug out," he paused. "Unfortunately they were stuck that way for a bit, we didn't find them right away."

"We are still working on getting it cleaned up enough to move, but even after that it's going to take time to get all of the dirt out of the hull."

There was silence in the group for several seconds before Colonel Erickson chimed in, "I'm still waiting for other theories."

Dr. Stone sat with his fingers steepled under his chin and added flatly, "Maybe we're dead."

This comment was met with silence from the rest of the group.

"Okay, well at least we have one working theory," the colonel said plainly. "Did any of you notice the full moon?"

A few nods around the table and Captain Pearce said, "Yes, it sure helped out with the recovery work until dawn came."

Erickson was surprised that none of them found this odd, but then so much had happened. Most people don't question or contemplate the sun or the moon. If the sun is up its day, and if it's down its night. The moon is either there or it isn't.

"There wasn't supposed to be a full moon last night, remember? We had clear skies but almost total darkness because it was a *new* moon," he said.

Erickson watched the others exchanged awkward glances as recollection spread across their faces. Except for Dr. Stone who was staring off into nowhere.

"I know this is a lot to take in, and none of it makes any sense. For now let's get our men focused on next steps," and the colonel laid out his plans.

Chapter 8: Gathering Party

Lieutenant Pontus sat in the passenger seat of a Humvee as it bounced along the uneven terrain in the cool morning air. He trusted the driver was trying to take it easy, but there was so much overgrown vegetation that it was impossible to predict where the easy path was, assuming there was one.

Pontus and his crew were 30 minutes out of Camp Nowhere, the name the men had bestowed upon the area of the valley the unit was hunkered down in. They were on a scouting mission but so far hadn't seen anything except tall grass and trees. They were looking for any sign of military or civilian personnel, even a North Korean tank would comforting at this point, and keeping an eye out for sources of food and water.

As they started moving up a rise, Pontus saw two small deer for an instant before they bolted into the brush.

At least there is something alive out here besides us, he thought, *something edible.*

"Take us the rest of the way up this ridge," Pontus instructed, "and we'll park it."

The four wheel drive vehicle climbed up the 50 foot ridge and into the sunshine with little effort and the driver parked it under a tree.

Once stopped, the four men got out and stretched. One by one, they gathered up their equipment, slung it onto their backs and grabbed their rifles. Then the lieutenant led the party down the other side of the ridge.

John Pontus was a 24 year old 1st Lieutenant starting his third year in the Army after graduating from West Point. While there he not only learned how to be an officer he also played football for three years, making first team as a senior. At six feet tall he had only average height for a college wide receiver, and not the kind of speed that would have anyone in professional football taking notice.

But John had good strength which had made him an effective run blocker for the Black Knight squad.

Looking out ahead of the group John could see that the terrain flattened out on the right, with a steep slope on the left. According to the paper map he had they would come upon a good sized river heading this direction. John decided to lead them along the base of the slope to keep them out of the exposed valley.

The small squad was keeping quiet to minimize their chances of being noticed. The silence and relative calm of their situation allowed Lt. Pontus to think more about their predicament. Since The Event two nights ago he had been working almost nonstop, but now his mind started to nibble on the puzzle.

Where is everything? Could the rest of the Corps have been destroyed? No way, and even if they had, where's all the wreckage? Maybe they had been attacked from the rear and had to maneuver to meet that threat?

John pondered this in the back of his mind while keeping himself and his men alert as they continued to look for signs of civilization.

* * *

Back at camp, Colonel Erickson sat in his tent with Dr. Stone drinking coffee.

"I have no rational explanation for what has happened here," the colonel said, an edge in his voice. "I know you've been mulling something over Damon. I want you to go ahead and spit it out, this dream doesn't seem to be going away."

Erickson saw the doctor's neutral expression change to what looked like a forced smile, no doubt the kind he used to break bad news to patients.

"Well, it does remain a possibility that I'm having a dream and all the rest of you are just figments of that false reality, but I don't think that to be the case," the doctor responded with a chuckle. "I'm afraid that it's not going to be that simple."

He stood and walked to a white board hanging on the tent wall, "If we take all the data we have and treat them as certainties, which we have no reason to do otherwise, then the evidence indicates that we are... out of place."

The doctor began drawing a diagram on the board, which the colonel quickly identified as a map of their position.

"This picture represents our state *prior* to the event. This circle is us, and these two lines represent the valley we were in. Immediately behind us is our path of advance, the torn up ground in our wake." The doctor drew lines representing this, then started to draw some other figures. "This is the rest of the regiment, over 200 armored vehicles and at least that many trucks and so forth in support. We were in direct physical proximity with this force, of course, as we are a subset of it."

Dr. Stone then drew some markings on the edges of his picture. "This represents the rest of the Corps assigned to the invasion, which we were in communication with, via satellite and wirelessly, prior to the flash. And this is the Air Force electronic jamming which we could detect at this same time," the doctor turned back to the colonel, "and I'm sure there are more similar examples if we talked to some of our other communications personnel, but you get the idea."

"Yes Doctor, I'm following you."

Stone moved to a clean area of the white board, "This is a picture of our state now." He drew the same circle labeled "us" and the two walls of the valley then stopped drawing.

"I don't think that it's everyone else that has gone away... It is *we* who are missing from this first picture," the doctor said flatly as he drew a line from the first picture to the second, "We have been relocated to a nearly identical physical location, but at a different point... in time."

The colonel grimaced and said doubtfully, "*In time?*"

"Yes, time. All the data points to it. Well, other than the fact that we don't know what mechanism has moved us through time and we don't know of any such technology existing on our world, certainly not by the Chinese or the Russians."

"Doctor, are you serious? I came to you for counsel because you've always had a rational scientific approach. Now you expect me to believe that we've somehow traveled across time?" the colonel said exasperated.

Erickson rubbed a hand over his tired face and calmed himself down.

"Okay, so that is your *theory*. How do we go about proving or disproving it?"

The doctor responded, "Ah, yes. Let's dismiss the indirect evidence, namely all the things that are missing from our perspective, although direct physical inspection of the location of the nearest city would be helpful."

"There should be evidence that some kind of force has acted upon us. Recall that our people and equipment aren't the only things that seem out of place here," the doctor hinted.

The colonel thought for a few seconds, "The grass?"

"Exactly," the doctor said. "And if you want specific evidence of time travel we have it. We know that at a *minimum* we have gone two weeks forward or backward because, as you pointed out, we went from a new moon to a full moon in a blink," Stone argued. "What's the difference between moving through time two weeks or two hundred years? We haven't the slightest idea how to do either. If one is possible, why not the other?"

Colonel Erickson responded, "Look Doctor, I don't have any other explanation for what happened, but you are talking about something out of a Crichton novel. I can't tell the men this theory. They'll think I'm crazy." Then he added, "At least not until we're sure I'm *not* crazy."

The doctor nodded his head, "I think that is the wise thing to do for now and I think we are likely to get more confirmation as the days go by."

31

The colonel stood, "I'm going to go take a look at our positions and see how the men are holding up." He took a step then turned back. "Assuming your theory is correct, what do we do?"

The doctor smiled, "That... is what I'm going to *start* thinking about."

* * *

Lt. Pontus sat on the hard ground looking at the river below him. They had come across it just before dark the previous day, too late in the day to investigate it properly. But with the dawn light the small waterway was taking shape and he could see the start of a path about 100 meters further downstream.

Perfect, he thought.

The lieutenant stifled a yawn then, lifting his helmet off his head, ran a hand over the dark brown stubble of his hair and decided it was morning.

"Alright, rise and shine boys," he said clearly.

The others began to stir one by one and John stood to stretch his stiff back and legs. The light was really taking effect now, he could see the valley clearly. Then something caught his eye... *movement*. He froze, then dropped slowly to his knees.

"Keep quiet, hold still," he whispered the order.

Lt. Pontus could make out the figures of three people coming down the trail below, each of them was carrying a large object. Reaching down he picked up his binoculars to get a closer look and saw three women in plain clothing, carrying large earthen pots.

His view was obscured by trees so he dropped down low and moved slowly downhill. He selected a spot offering concealment that had a good view of where the path met the water, where he assumed they were going.

He got the three women back into view and gave them a closer inspection. All three appeared to be Asian, with dark black hair tied back. One was taller than the other two and as she set her pot down next to the river, she looked up and back in his general direction, giving him a good look at her face. Her features were sharp, almost chiseled, whereas the other two appeared to have softer round faces. She and the others looked to be young no more than 20.

Their clothes were worn and dingy made of a woven fabric. They reminded him of pictures he had seen of people living in third world countries, simple, drab coverings. Each in turn stooped down to draw water from the river. Then they started heading back down the trail carrying their water.

The lieutenant moved slowly back up the hill to tell the others what he had seen. Then he selected Private Cushman.

"You and me, we'll follow them. Leave your gear and rifle here. You two stay here and we'll contact you every within an hour."

The women were nearly out of sight now, down around a bend. Lt. Pontus and Private Cushman kept low and started moving. As the women went out of sight, they risked noise and moved quickly to close the gap.

As they pair reached the bend, still uphill from the trail, the private said, "Smell that?"

The lieutenant paused and then gave a nod, it was the distinct smell of wood burning. They slowed down and moved around the corner of the hill. As they did so they saw the three women with their pots and further ahead, a village.

John scanned the village with his binoculars and saw perhaps 30 small crude structures with what appeared to be thatched roofs. At the far end he could see some livestock in a small corral. But he didn't see any vehicles and the only light was coming from two stone fire pits.

"This place is seriously rural," John said to the private. "I knew things in the North were tough but I didn't know there were people living in huts. Radio the others and tell them that we've found civilization."

Chapter 9: What Butterflies?

Colonel Erickson looked at Dr. Stone, seated across the table from him.

"Well Major," the colonel began, "earlier today one of our scout teams found an inhabited village about ten or fifteen kilometers from here. So I ask again, what do we do? There is no sign of technology in the village, so nothing to disprove your time travel theory... yet."

The doctor smiled, "I don't expect that any will be found."

It seemed to the colonel that the doctor was happy with that prospect. Starting with their previous meeting he'd noticed that the doctor's typically even, at times dour, demeanor had become much brighter, almost excited.

The doctor stood and spoke in a manner that reminded the colonel of a college professor giving a lecture.

"Bill, I've been mulling over our predicament since we spoke yesterday. There is no precedent for this, well that we know of," a big smile. "I have only scant knowledge regarding the theory of relativity and the like. So, sadly I've had to reflect back on works of fiction and think about the scenarios presented, then considered how they apply to us."

He continued, "Let us assume that we have gone *backward* in time rather than forward, all the evidence points to this," he paused. "One of the most familiar concepts around going backwards in time is the butterfly effect."

"I've heard of it," the colonel said.

The doctor continued, "Essentially the theory is if you go back in time and change something, even a small insignificant thing, it could make a huge impact on the future, our past, always with dire consequences if you believe the fictional accounts. So the protagonists usually try to keep a low profile until they are returned to their own time, which is another common aspect to these stories."

"So you think we need to hold up and just wait until we can get back to our own time?" the colonel asked.

The doctor replied flatly, "Not at all sir."

"Unlike a work of fiction made for entertainment purposes, there isn't any reason to assume that our predicament will have a tidy happy conclusion."

"We have no idea what mechanism sent us back in time, but the most likely cause is located back in our former time. As such, we shouldn't suppose that this same mechanism will reach across time and act upon us again. If it was a freak event of space and time, then why would it occur again at all, let alone act upon us once again? If it was done *purposely* by some intelligent force, then clearly they wanted us to come here. I can't think of any reason they would have for then bringing us back, even if they could," he stated.

Erickson had seen and read some of the fiction too and he had been holding out hope that the doctor would come up with a reason to think that they would be able to get back to their time. While that does make for a happy story, the reality of their situation was setting in, there was no reason to expect a fairy tale ending.

"I think we should resign ourselves to the fact that this is our new existence and we should start getting settled. We should make contact with this village and start learning more about *this* time. We'll need to create a place to live, establish a long term source of food and so on. It's not unlike being a colony in a new world," the doctor said.

"What about the butterfly effect?" the colonel countered.

"Ah, that is a trickier matter to disprove. As I said I think we should start settling here, so I'm of the opinion that we don't need to be concerned with the butterfly effect. I believe that this time we are in, while like our past, is not actually *our* past. We existed, based on our history, if our history changed and we didn't exist, how then would we have been able to change our own history?" he reasoned. "I think this is a new, or parallel time to our own."

"A parallel time?" the colonel questioned.

"Yes Colonel, there are theories which propose that there isn't just one path through time. Starting with the origin of the universe, suppose that there are ten versions of the universe all happening simultaneously. We are only aware of our own existence, but there are nine other paths through time all running their course independently.

"The events in each timeline could be almost identical, or they could differ because of decisions or events that are somewhat random or happen at slightly different times," Dr. Stone explained.

The colonel nodded trying to take it all in, "Okay, so if we've shifted to a parallel timeline, why are we hundreds of years in the past? Why aren't we at a similar time to the one we left?"

The doctor cocked his head, "Excellent question Colonel." He walked to the whiteboard and lifted a marker. "There are two distinct possibilities I can think of right off. First, it could be that the people in this time did not progress at the same rate as in our time. A plague at the wrong time or some other delay in societal evolution could have slowed their development.

"However, I think it likely that, while these timelines are parallel, perhaps it would be more accurate to say moving together, they don't necessarily move at the same rate through time and space," the doctor drew a series of concentric arcs, the shape of a rainbow.

"Instead of moving along in straight lines, think of the timelines as moving along together like a wave. If we look at a segment of the wave, just a crest for example it is a series of bands that are congruent, but are of unequal length," Dr. Stone explained.

He then drew a line straight down through the waveform, "This represents where time is at, the 'Now ' if you will, through all the timelines."

"Let me propose that the time we are from is this middle band here," the doctor marked an X on the line where it passed through the middle band of the rainbow. "From where the wave begins over here to where I've drawn the "now" line is a distance of 10 units. The distance to the Now Line in the next band down is only 9, while the band above us has a length of 11," the doctor paused. "Do you follow me Colonel?"

Colonel Erickson was keeping up and thinking that Dr. Stone would indeed make a good professor. "Yes, I'm with you so far."

"Good. Now that I've demonstrated that these parallel timelines are of unequal length, let's put it in terms of years. Along the middle band of the wave, let's call it 'Our Time', think of it as a length of 15,000 years. The band below ours, the world we find ourselves in at present, is shorter in length and thus may have only experienced 12,000 years. So by moving to this other timeline, we will have effectively gone backward in time 3,000 years," the doctor concluded.

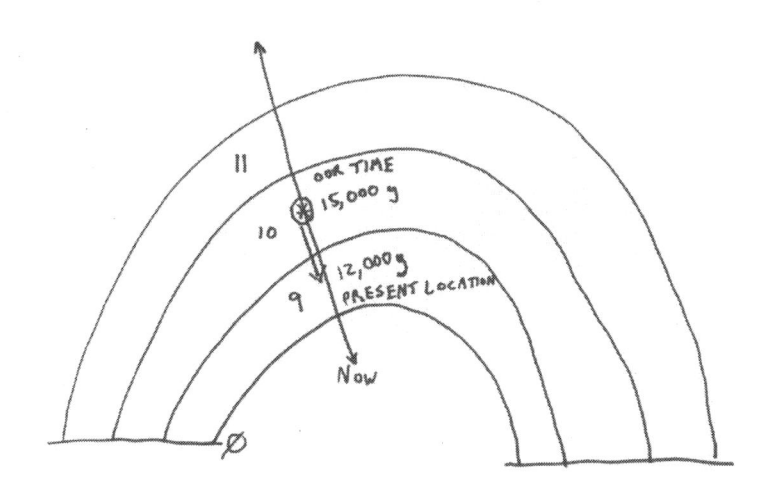

Doctor Stone's white board diagram

The colonel thought it through, and though it seemed unreal, he had no other explanation for what had happened.

"So, in your theory, is there a way to get back up to our correct timeline?" the colonel asked hopefully.

"In theory yes, but I'm afraid that is all it is right now. We still don't know how we were transported to this timeline, or how we would move forward rather than backward in time. I'm sorry Colonel, I find this very fascinating intellectually and it is a possible explanation as to how we got here. But I don't know how to utilize it to help us," Damon Stone said apologetically.

"Okay, then let's get back to practical matters. What should we do now that we are here?" the colonel asked, frustrated with the ambiguity of it all.

"Yes Colonel," the doctor agreed. "I still think that we should come to grips with our situation and accept that this is our new home and start getting acclimated. Making contact with this village and learning all we can about our new world should be our top priority. Let's not worry about what effect our actions will have on the future of this time.

"If you want to think about it another way, we are here so unless you want to condemn the rest of us to death we *will* start making an impact on our surroundings almost immediately. Just the fact that our vehicles and technology are here will change anyone who sees them. Unless you know how to make the whole unit disappear without a trace?" the doctor concluded.

The colonel thought about it, "That would be tough…"

…*but* not *impossible.*

* * *

Lieutenant Pontus and Private Cushman had been observing the village for half the day. They had moved to different locations to try and get a better view but were concerned about being spotted and so didn't move in closer. Their orders were explicit about not making contact.

John started looking around the hill they were on taking in the flowers and new buds on the trees, and made a realization.

"It's spring," he said calmly.

Cushman looked to his lieutenant, "Spring? Didn't we cross the border on 7 August?"

"Yes we did."

John had been taking notes on what they saw, so far it was what he would expect of a third world village. They had seen mostly women doing various chores like preparing food and washing clothes in the river. Others worked in fields along both sides of the river. Several small children were helping with the chores but also running around and playing from time to time.

The villagers had made many more trips down the trail to get water, all by women and children.

Pontus turned to Private Cushman, "Go and head back to the others, send Jenkins back with more food and water."

The private nodded and said, "Yes, sir," as he turned to go.

Some activity nearby caught John's eye and he lifted the binoculars to get a better look. He saw three women walking together on the path, but they stopped short of his position and moved toward the river. He hadn't seen anyone at this particular location before. It was between the place where they gathered water and the spot that seemed to be designated for cleaning clothes.

The women were each carrying folded cloths and set them down on a waist high rock. As he got a better look he realized that it was the three young women he had seen that morning, the tall one and her two friends.

He made a quick note on paper. As he returned to observing he saw the two shorter women were doing something... they moved down to the water and... disrobed.

Crap

Pontus broke off his gaze. He was conflicted by his conscience, which told him he should be embarrassed, and his mind which was telling him he was missing a chance to get more information about their situation.

He shook off the mixture of emotions and told himself to grow up. He lifted his binoculars again and tried to make his observations in a detached manner.

The two shorter women were naked but for a cloth wrapped around the hips. Physically they were slim but not skinny, and kind of straight through the hips like a man. They walked down into the water, where he lost sight of them. From his brief view of their bodies he surmised they were healthy.

Now the tall one approached the water and as she began to remove her clothes he found that his heart was racing. She stood bare, but for the same loin cloth. Compared to the other two her shoulders were more pronounced and she was narrower in the waist. The result was a beautiful hourglass figure. Then she too walked down and out of sight into the water.

Even though he couldn't see them anymore, he felt flushed. He lowered his binoculars and self-consciously looked around. He looked down at his notes and decided they were sufficient as is.

The women weren't in the water long before getting out. He saw them get dressed and feeling both relieved and embarrassed again, lifted his binoculars. The clothes they were wearing now were the same type as what they had taken off.

Then they started walking back down the trail toward the village.

John watched until they were out of sight. Then he closed his eyes and allowed himself a moment of rest. As he did so a face flashed through his mind, the face... of the tall one.

*   *   *

Colonel Erickson and his unit commanders listened as Dr. Stone explained his theory to them. That they had gone back in time, and the course of action he and the colonel had discussed.

At first, Erickson had observed the others looking at the doctor as if he were insane, then they began to look down or away, clearly not believing. As he had gone on and walked them through all the indicators that supported his theory, and no other as of yet, their expressions grew sullen.

"As crazy as it seems, it's the best explanation we have for our situation," the colonel said. "Even if you don't believe it, fact is we are cutoff in Middle-of-Nowhere, Korea. We lack sufficient fuel to get far and where would we go? Our food and water supply is dwindling fast, so we need to get about the business of surviving."

Major Baker said, "Do you want to tell the men this theory? Besides hurting morale, in the longer term it'll lead to a breakdown of discipline, or do you plan to disband and tell everyone to just do as they wish?"

Lieutenant Colonel Brower, Erickson's second in command, nodded and in his deep voice said, "I agree. But we have to tell them something."

Colonel Erickson said, "I don't want to keep it from the men, I think they have a right to know. But I don't want to tell them until we have a plan for what we are going to do so we can focus them on that. Building a place to live and establishing food and water supplies are first and foremost."

Erickson noticed his officers perk up at talk of this more practical matter.

"As to disbanding, as time wears on maybe but for now, we need to maintain order and discipline," Erickson added.

"Do you plan to build right here?" Captain James asked.

"Not necessarily," Erickson replied. "We've got maps that are still fairly accurate as to the terrain, and we've sent scouts out in several directions. I think we should identify some possibilities and pick the best."

"I want us to make contact with the village northeast of here," the colonel said. "We'll take a small team in, no firearms, battle dress uniforms," Erickson said.

41

Dr. Stone chimed in, "I would like to be a part of this team. I want to assess the condition of the people, and look for signs of diseases we need to be concerned about."

The colonel nodded, "You are at the top of my list. You, myself, and Lieutenant Pontus. I'm also going to invite Ms. Carlisle, our embedded reporter, along for a different perspective. As luck would have it none of our fluent Korean speakers made it here with us, though that may not have helped anyway."

"We'll head out this afternoon and link up with the observation post, and go in tomorrow morning. The rest of you keep your people busy. I hope to be prepared to present our plan to them within the next couple of days. Dismissed," Erickson concluded.

Chapter 10: First Contact

The sun had been up for two hours but Lieutenant Pontus had been up all night.

The previous evening Colonel Erickson had come up to the observation post and given him a briefing on their mission to make contact with the village. That's when the colonel had dropped the bombshell on him. *We've gone backwards in time?* It had taken a while to sink in, was still sinking in. John had dwelled on the possibility that they were in a different time for most of the night. His mind wouldn't let it go, chewing on it over and over, but not getting anywhere.

His long night was catching up to him now as he felt sleepiness creeping in. But then he heard a noise behind him, and turned to see Colonel Erickson, Major Stone and a woman he didn't know walking up to his position. Trailing behind them were two members of his patrol. Strangely the colonel and major were wearing only green t-shirts with their camouflage pants. Pontus stood to greet them.

Colonel Erickson said, "Good morning Lieutenant."

"Good morning sir."

"Lieutenant, you remember Major Stone?"

Dr. Stone extended a hand, which Lt. Pontus clasped with a firm shake, "Yes of course. Good morning sir," he said.

Erickson motioned to the woman, "Have you met Ms. Carlisle? She is the reporter embedded with our unit."

She offered her hand as well, which John took with more care.

"Please call me Renee," she said. Her bright blue eyes lit up as she spoke.

"Nice to meet you," then answering the colonel he said, "I knew we had a reporter but no we hadn't met until now."

Renee was tall and slender, a few years older than he. Her hair was pulled back making it easy to see her sharp attractive facial features. It made sense that she was on television John reasoned. Then he noticed that she was wearing a fair amount of makeup which he thought odd given the circumstances.

Doctor Stone spoke, "Lieutenant how are you handling the news of our predicament?"

"It's hard to accept. But it would explain how come it's spring now, when a couple days ago it was summer," he replied.

The doctor looked around at the bushes and then gave a beaming smile, like he'd just won a bet.

Colonel Erickson said, "Any action this morning?"

Pontus responded, "They had a water detail about 30 minutes ago, and there will likely be more of those soon. Nothing else."

"Let's head in, hopefully we won't meet up with anyone on the trail. You have the package lieutenant?" the colonel asked.

"Yes sir," he replied lifting a small backpack, which he slung over his shoulder.

"Let's proceed."

"Sir, I'd like it if Private Cushman joined us. I'm not really expecting trouble, but I'd rather have an extra body on hand just in case," Pontus said.

"Fine Lieutenant."

Erickson spoke to the group, "Remember, smile, be friendly, don't make sudden movements. We'll figure out a way to communicate and hopefully we can establish friendly relations." Then he instructed, "Lieutenant, Private, ditch your jackets and helmets. We don't want to look too imposing."

John complied with the order but said, "Sir, I still want to bring my sidearm, holstered of course."

"Yes Lieutenant, I think that's prudent," the colonel replied.

Then as a group they walked down to the trail. John took up position at the back of the loose column so he could keep everyone else in view.

The group soon closed the distance with the village and its smells and sounds came alive. John realized now that he hadn't heard much talking from the villagers he'd observed on the path. Now the unmistakable sound of voices carried out to them, in a language he was unfamiliar with.

So far they hadn't been noticed and were only 75 meters from the village. Then a man standing near a hut turned and looked at them. Lieutenant Pontus heard the man calling out to someone, not in alarm, but with a sense of urgency which made him a little nervous. In the time he had been observing the village, he had seen no weapons, but that didn't mean they didn't have any.

They were almost in the village now and John could see a fire pit straight ahead, smoldering dully. The man, perhaps in his 40s, walked forward and stood waiting to meet them. He was short to John's eyes, about five feet and a few inches, but taller than many of the other villagers present. Then others, a mix of men and women, drew near and around the first man and watched them walk the last several meters to the village where the colonel stopped a short distance away from their greeter.

To his right, John saw two young males walk up. The shorter, younger one was carrying a large stick and the other held a crude metal sword. The boys held their weapons loosely at their sides, watching.

Colonel Erickson held out an open hand and spoke, "Hello, An nyoung ha seh yo," which John knew to be a greeting in Korean.

The first man looked at him curiously and replied with something that sounded like a question. Then another man, smaller in stature than the first, walked up to join the group, he was older still, probably 50 or more. He took a central position opposite the colonel who repeated his greeting.

The second man replied with a short phrase, and then a longer one, which again sounded like a question.

Colonel Erickson tried again, pantomiming as he spoke slowly, "We have come from the other side of that mountain."

The old man, with his scraggly white beard asked another question, maybe the same one as before.

The colonel beckoned, "Lieutenant."

Pontus turned so that the colonel could access his backpack. From it he pulled two large water bottles. After he took them out he slowly walked toward the old man smiling and offering them out to him, motioning that he should take them.

The older man looked surprised but reached out to take one as the first man walked up and examined the second bottle suspiciously. But that only lasted an instant, then they became fascinated, turning them over and watching the liquid and air bubbles swish around. The old man tapped the plastic bottle and then touched it to his mouth. He then said something to the first man, clearly delighted. He said something very pleasantly to the colonel.

Erickson took a step forward and unscrewed the lid, took it off, then showed them that it screwed back on, he then removed it from the bottle and handed it to the old man. This began a new round of fascination as he placed the cap on and tentatively turned it back and forth then took it off again.

John found this amusing, he was glad that their present was being well received. He watched as the leader tipped the bottle and poured some of the water onto his hand, which he then licked. He nodded his approval, but John surmised that the bottles themselves were much more interesting to them than the contents.

The other people around began to smile. The leader said a few words to his people, and they had a chuckle. He then turned and said something to the five new comers with a smile. The one thing John could discern was one of the words he used to refer to himself, "Kuson."

Erickson extended a hand and the man looked at it, then extended his own and clasped it in what wasn't really a hand shake, but close enough.

Then it began, the men and women approached them readily and examined them closely. They were all quite short on average, around five feet tall more or less, the men and women of similar height. They reached out hands to feel their clothes, their skin, and one man examined the colonel's dusty boots with awe.

John found it a little embarrassing, but understandable. Clearly they had not seen white men or women before, or any sort of modern clothing. At this point the first man noticed the handle of John's combat knife and touched it. The man asked John a question, which he could easily guess.

The colonel nodded and said, "Let him have a look Lieutenant."

John slipped the knife up and out of its sheath and handed it to the man, who looked at it with wonder. He held it in his hands like it was Excalibur, and started talking nonstop to himself to the others and to John. Then he walked over to a nearby log.

"Be careful, it's very sharp," John cautioned, trying to convey the message with raised hands, his tone and facial expression.

The man paid no attention and grazed it across the surface of the wood, taking out a small chunk. He smiled and now gripped it as a tool. He turned to John and was emphatic about something. He started pointing around the village in general, then to the knife.

"I think he wants to buy it from you Lieutenant," Dr. Stone chuckled. "Make sure you get something good for it."

John smiled, *this is going well*.

"Yes," he nodded.

The man seemed to understand and beamed. He said something, motioned for John to stay put, then ran off.

47

Others from the village came out. John guessed that their arrival must be the most exciting thing that had happened to these people in years. Life appeared hard, drab and monotonous in the village.

Pontus saw the doctor engage in a 'conversation' with Kuson, the village leader. He was trying to explain something. Then he noticed a small child, a girl perhaps five, standing near them alongside a woman. The doctor was pointing to the girl's hand. She appeared a little scared, but the doctor was putting on his best bedside manner, kneeling down low to be at eye level with her. With her mother's encouragement the girl lifted her hand. John could see that one of her fingers was red and swollen.

As some of the villagers left to go back to whatever they had been doing, still more came. It was then that John noticed three young women walk up behind the leader Kuson, three women he had seen before.

The *tall one* he could see now wasn't so tall, perhaps five foot six, but her friends were under five feet. The leader turned to them and said something, then motioned to the colonel and the doctor, introductions of some kind. John found himself walking over, having to push through some men who were talking to him and continuing to inspect his every button.

As he got near, the three women looked up at him and he locked eyes with the tall one for a moment. Her hair was dusty and windblown, but her light brown eyes were moist and alive. Up close now he found her to be... *beautiful*. John noticed that his heart was beating faster, which surprised him. She didn't say anything and her gaze moved back to Kuson and the colonel who were trying to converse.

John broke off his stare as he felt someone tugging on him. Turning he saw it was one of the teen boys, now without his sword. He was actually tugging at the holster on John's right hip. The boy asked him a question pointing to the holster.

John smiled but put his hand over the holster and said, "No, not this one," shaking his head.

The boy persisted, pointing and talking. John maintained his approach and waved his hands back and forth over the holstered pistol. The boy grimaced and slowly drifted back and away.

The lieutenant heard a voice shouting, it was the first man coming back. As he looked closer, John saw that he was leading a small goat by a rope.

Oh no.

The man walked right up, knife in one hand and goat in the other. He motioned for John to take the rope.

The colonel was looking on and said, "Looks like a good deal, take it."

"Yes sir," Lt. Pontus said meekly.

He reached out to take the rope that was tied to the small brown goat. The man was all smiles and two other men came to examine his newly purchased knife.

"Lieutenant, give him two knives for that," the doctor instructed. "The goat is very valuable to him and the knife means very little to us. I don't want to set a precedent that takes advantage of them."

That made sense to John. He turned to find Cushman and saw him looking at the wall of one of the small structures with some men from the village.

"Private, give me your knife."

"Sir?" came his reply, but he walked over, pulled out his knife and gave it to him handle first.

John walked over to the goat's *former* owner and handed him the second knife. He seemed confused at first, but John held up two fingers next to the knife and pointed at the goat. An appreciative smile crept over the man's face as he made the connection, taking the knife. The other men standing near him immediately started badgering him.

Looks like he's going to make out pretty good on the deal, John thought with a smile.

Chapter 11: G Troop

Colonel Erickson sat in his tent as the cool of the night crept in along with the smell of coming rain. It had been a long and tiring day meeting with the villagers for the first time. Trying to communicate, to convey even the simplest concepts, was very difficult across the language and cultural barrier and it had taken a lot out of him.

One victory in communication was establishing the words for "day" "night" "sun" and the concept of the passing of one day. Establishing better communication was one of his highest priorities. The village was small, only about 100 to 150 people he estimated, and he had around 500 men and women currently under his command. He was torn as to whether he should try to teach his soldiers the local language, or the villagers English. With the doctor's encouragement he decided to try and teach a few of the villagers English to use as interpreters as a start. That was something the colonel wanted to discuss with the village elder, Kuson, tomorrow.

Erickson thought that the meeting had gone well, hardly could have been better. The others in the little greeting party had confirmed that this was their impression as well. In addition to exchanging a few items, including a goat of all things, the doctor had administered some medication and treatment for infections and minor skin rashes and fungi. The doctor said he'd like to see every single villager, if they were willing, for at least a cursory examination, fingers, toes and other likely troublesome spots. Another thing to convey to their leader.

But before that, the colonel had another important matter to attend to. He needed to tell his men that they were in a new time, essentially a new world, and that they would likely never see any of their friends or family again. He wasn't sure how to handle dropping such weighty and hard to believe news on such a large group of people, it was weighing on him.

He would tell the officers first in a separate meeting so that they would be prepared to help the men and women cope with the news. He would also ask the officers to keep a close eye on their people over time to see if any of them were having trouble adjusting to their new life.

A new life, Dr. Stone described it as starting a new colony. What could he do to motivate them? The short term stuff was easy, food, water, shelter, but what after that? There were only 13 women in the unit, plus the reporter, so the prospect of family was limited by available resources.

He then made a mental note not to refer to the women as "resources."

William Erickson, at 45 years of age, had never been married. As a career army officer he'd always been very focused and driven by the work. He had found he was good at the job and had advanced steadily, even without being overly political.

Even with the increasing level of integration and number of females in the military over the previous two decades, he'd never met anyone that he'd become close to. Nor had he met many women that it would be appropriate for him to be close to given regulations.

Thinking back to the issue of lack of available women, he thought of the village. He had noticed a lot of women of various ages, but not as many men. Had they been working away from the village or hunting? Something else to ask about. But still, the number of people in the village was low, and he couldn't have almost 500 men descending on it en masse.

The same was true of exchanging goods with the villagers. In their excitement about all the new and wondrous things the twenty-first century had to offer them, they might give away too much and actually hinder themselves. Regulation of not only trade but of how many of his soldiers should be allowed to visit the village at one time was needed.

Damn, I've become a bureaucrat.

*   *   *

John Pontus was in camp and had just eaten his first hot lunch in days. Now in his tent, he was gathering up some basic items, like a toothbrush and shaving kit, to take with him back to the observation post near the village.

After gathering his things he sat for a moment and thought about his parents, and wondered what they were thinking. John wasn't sure how things looked back in the *real* world. *They must think we were killed or captured.* He wasn't sure how long that news would take to get back to his family and his girlfriend Kathryn.

"Hey John, way to go buddy," came a voice from outside his tent.

John turned and saw Lt. Norman, leader of 3rd Scout Platoon.

"Lance, oh... uh, thanks," he replied, not really sure what his counterpart was getting at. John walked out of the tent to face him.

"You met the locals, you're hanging out with the colonel. Good stuff," he said but without much sincerity in his voice.

Lt. Pontus shrugged, "It was interesting meeting the villagers."

Lt. Norman was already looking away, not listening to John's reply. Then his eyes fixed on something on the ground next to them.

"You know, since G Troop is missing in action I think we should form a new one around you, Goat Troop," Lance laughed at his own joke then turned and walked off.

Lt. Pontus looked down at the small brown animal tied to the trunk of a nearby tree where it was contentedly eating leaves and branches.

John just shook his head. *You're such an ass Norman.*

53

Chapter 12: Doctor Stone

Major Damon Stone, Doctor of Medicine, sat in the dimly lit tent that served as his office and clinic. It was dark outside and his only source of light was a fuel powered lantern, a luxury few were allowed. The open door flaps provided ample ventilation but made the room somewhat cool. Dr. Stone didn't mind this, it helped him think.

Like so many others in the unit who had found themselves out of their own time, Dr. Stone was reflecting on what had been lost. However, he was *focused* on what had been gained.

Things couldn't be better.

Damon Stone was a brilliant man, but not the most self-disciplined. Problems seemed to follow him around. He had volunteered for active duty, having already been a reservist, in order to escape some legal trouble.

But now he had escaped *all* of his problems. Chief among them the bitter ex-wife who was never satisfied with what she could squeeze out of him. She was a tall, beautiful blonde but her nature was like November rain. While working at the Chicago area hospital near his home in Lincoln Park, he had told a petite resident that kissing his wife was like having a cold fish swim around in his mouth. He had found the resident's tongue to be much warmer and accommodating. His wife had found out, and thus was his ex.

Then there was all the debt they had amassed, made worse by his penchant for going to Las Vegas, sometimes on business, others times pleasure, but always to gamble. It was his *one vice* he always told himself. If his wife could spend thousands of dollars on breasts, that he rarely got to see, he could drop as much entertaining himself under the bright lights in Sin City.

Now those, and a few *minor* things, were all in the past. Before him now was a world that was going to be his oyster, once he could find civilization. Damon wasn't sure what the year was, but he reasoned they were in the bronze era for this region.

While making contact with the village the day before he had noticed that they possessed nothing made of iron or steel, only bronze. Korea in ancient times was fairly remote, but still he reasoned they must be no further along than 500 B.C. and more likely 1,000 B.C. or earlier. He would need more data to be certain.

Once he had convinced himself that his theory of going back in time was correct Dr. Stone had been quick to realize the benefits. He was currently the most knowledgeable person *in the world.* When it came to medicine and biology, most certainly, but also to many fundamentals of science like chemistry. Certainly there were others in the world with more raw intelligence, but no one had his intellect combined with his knowledge and training, nor his medications, and he was certain he could parlay that into wealth and power for himself, and any that wished to assist him. He wasn't selfish after all.

It would take time though, it would take patience. First, he needed to learn the local language well enough to be able to speak for himself. He needed to do that prior to making contact with someone important, a king or an emperor, someone that he could impress with his abilities and that could reward him for access to his knowledge.

He'd also need to recruit some of the soldiers to join him. Not only for protection, but also to put on a show of force to impress would be patrons, if the situation required it.

Fate had dealt Damon Stone an interesting hand and he intended to make the most of it. As he had this thought, he frowned, puzzled. *It's not fate, something brought us here.*

He had no references or theories to go off of but those from movies, TV, books. *What was it they had in common?* He was sure he was forgetting something simple.

Let's see, Star Trek, faster than light travel. Back to the Future, plutonium or a lightning bolt to fuel the device, he recalled.

Many different sources had a "time machine" of sorts, but many of those didn't even try to explain their mechanism of operation. *The Final Countdown, a mysterious and powerful storm.*

Ah, and there it was. So simple he was overlooking it as obvious, but of course, there was one element that would be absolutely necessary for time travel.

A massive amount of energy.

* * *

The next morning, Dr. Stone headed out promptly with the sun. He carried not only a shovel but several boards each a meter long and a bag of other items. He walked south west, back up the valley in the direction that the unit had come from.

Damon Stone's pale skin glowed in the bright morning sun. He had a fair complexion and his hair was in the midst of transitioning from blond to white, but he could only blame so much on genetics. He knew he didn't get outside enough and was looking forward to today's excursion.

It only took about ten minutes to get to his objective, the location where he and the rest of the unit had first arrived in this time. It was around a kilometer from the camp and importantly wasn't visible from there.

As he arrived at the location, Dr. Stone looked around to gain his bearings on what vehicles had been where. There were deep ruts all around him, surrounded by mounds of dirt from where each one had been dug out. He kept walking until he came to the last sets of ruts.

Stone set down his equipment and pulled out a map and a list of which units had arrived and which were missing. He walked back and forth across the valley, noting the specific locations of the last vehicle in each formation that made the trip across time.

Analyzing the locations on his map, it made a rough line across the valley. The doctor smiled, *Excellent.*

He retrieved his shovel and started on the north side of the valley, in the pit which used to contain an M1 tank. From there he walked several meters behind where the tank had sat and started to dig a hole in the ground.

It took him several minutes of hard work, but then as he brought up shovel after shovel of brown dirt, suddenly there was green. The doctor confirmed that what he was seeing was grass then he walked several more meters away and started digging a new hole.

It too had a layer of grass a couple feet down so the doctor wondered if he should move a further distance away before digging his next hole. He surveyed the ground trying to divine where to dig and noticed an oddity. The grass and weeds were tall, 18 inches or more in places. But about 30 feet away there was a gap in the pattern of the grass, it was regular in shape like a narrow slot.

Dr. Stone approached and saw that the hole was indeed devoid of grass in a space about six inches wide and six feet long. Reaching down he felt a cool metal object, it was round like a pipe. He lifted up on the end of the heavy object and was staring down the barrel of an M1 tank's 120mm cannon.

Setting it down, Stone went to the other end and hefted it. The barrel had been cut by something, bare metal was exposed and the surface looked like it had been coarse sanded. The doctor chuckled and said, "Excellent!"

Dr. Stone set it back down and pulled a marker flag out of his bag. He stuck the stiff wire into the ground next to the barrel's severed end.

He walked across the valley to the next mound of dirt where a vehicle had been dug out.

If only the remaining points will be so easy to plot.

Chapter 13: Fast Lane Ends Here

Though Renee made only sparse comments in her notebook while interviewing people she did make extensive use of it as a journal. Her real journal was safe back at home in Malibu. She hadn't wanted to risk losing it in on this mission, but she realized the joke was on her as she would never see it again.

Date: unknown, Day 7 since The Event

Just returned from Colonel Erickson's speech to his men. He told them the crazy time travel business, which I still can't believe myself, and I've had four days to think it over. A bunch of the guys chuckled quietly when the colonel broke the news. He's a calm man, but can really get everyone's attention when he needs to. I like him. He really has a knack for dealing with his guys. He let them know he was serious but without being harsh or watering down the news, he's a really good communicator.

But this place is so boring. Going to the village a couple of days ago has still been the highlight of the week. There is nothing to do here and since I'm not part of the army, I'm left out of having any responsibilities.

It was nice of Colonel Erickson to give me this private tent, just like most of his officers, but now I kind of wish I'd been put with Sal, then at least I'd have someone to talk to and get included. Ugh! I'm the popular and fun one, but there isn't a way to show that here. Sal is so nice, she stops by to check on me. But I guess she's officially off of babysitter duty since we aren't in a war anymore.

Someone is outside my tent...

Renee laid down the spiral notebook and called out, "Hello?"

"Ms. Carlisle," came a familiar voice, "its Lance Norman."

She rolled her eyes. Attracting jerks had been a lifelong curse. Then she smiled to herself, well she attracted all kinds of guys.

"Yes Lieutenant, come in," she purposely did not use his name.

He stopped by almost daily it seemed. The camp sites were arranged by unit and since she had been riding with Norman's platoon, his tent was close by.

The lieutenant slipped in through the door opening and stood, a look of concern on his face.

"I just wanted to check in on you and make sure you were adjusting okay after the colonel's big announcement. A lot of the guys were hit hard, and I just wanted to see how you were doing," he said softly.

It would have been a very nice and considerate gesture on his part, if it were true.

She stood up and, as she was still wearing her boots, was slightly taller than he.

"Thanks Lieutenant, that's nice but not necessary. I mean the news is shocking, but I was briefed on it a few days ago, before we went into the village," she said pleasantly.

The news registered visually on Norman's face as a slight sinking of his chin.

"Oh, okay, right," he tried to recover. "Well, I'm still right around the corner if you want to talk about it, or anything else related to our situation here."

"Thanks, I'll keep that in mind," she said with a forced smile. He waited a moment then retreated out of her tent.

Renee sat back down on her chair, a luxury item, and returned to her journal. But since she was concerned about privacy, made only a quick mention of the lieutenant's visit.

She had received quite a bit of attention from the men the last couple of days, and she predicted it would only increase now with the colonel's announcement. The most forward were Lance, whom she couldn't stand, and another officer whose name and rank escaped her. He at least had been pleasant and wasn't unattractive.

She had been thinking about what it would mean if they truly were orphaned in this time. It didn't take a math major to figure out that the ratio of men to women was terribly lopsided, at least 20 to 1. Once the men figured that out they would be lining up to get an edge on the competition.

She smiled and thought, *it's a woman's world.*

The only man who had actually caught *her* eye thus far had been Lieutenant Pontus, John, whom she had met on the trip into the village. He was tall, quiet and hadn't flirted with her, which really got her attention. Though he was a few years her younger he really pushed all of her buttons. Besides being confident and handsome his eyes had that smoldering look, like David Boreanaz of *Angel* fame.

Back in the life now left behind, she'd been seeing the same man since her arrival in LA. Bob Nasworthy, several years her senior, who was a producer at the network. He was ruggedly handsome, the way she liked men, but was all LA. So he wasn't really rugged, it was just a look, everyone in LA had a look. But that was fine, Renee had chosen a life of perception over reality many years earlier.

Bob was well connected outside of the network which had given her the chance to parade around on someone's huge yacht with all of the other beautiful people. For many, socializing on such an occasion was a means to an end. But living life on a billionaire's yacht *was* an end to Renee, she just needed to figure out how to find someone to say she could stay, or at least not mind her visiting every day.

Bob had told her on that occasion that he loved the high cut of her white designer one-piece. But she hadn't worn it for him, she'd worn it as bait hoping to attract someone with, at minimum, an eight figure bank account.

Renee shook away the memories, meaningless and useless here. Bob had been a surprisingly good guy and she had ended up liking him more than intended. But she hadn't loved him and now that she wouldn't see him again didn't have any regrets.

What she *did* regret was taking this assignment which had dropped her into the quiet hell of this valley!

Renee tossed her journal aside and leaned over, supporting her brow with the tips of her fingers, trying to breath slow and deep.

She'd been keeping up the pleasantries and appearances, mostly for herself, but she sensed it coming to an end. With nothing to fuel or numb her daily existence, the grip she maintained on her psyche was starting to slip. Sometimes her chest was tight with panic and she thought she might completely lose control. Through all of this she wasn't even sure what it was that she was keeping in check. But she did know that she'd kept it in there for years and wanted it to stay put.

* * *

Private Murphy lay on a cot in the small medical clinic in Camp Nowhere, his stomach tied up, calf muscles twisted and brow on fire. He hadn't felt sick like this since he was a little kid. What bothered him almost as much as the physical symptoms was the knowledge that he had done it to himself.

A medic approached with water and a pill.

"This is just to help with the symptoms, the doctor will have to figure out what else to give you," he said.

Matt took the pill and as much water as he thought he could keep down.

"Believe it or not, it could be worse. There was a guy in here yesterday, Private Curtis, he was puking like he'd downed a fifth of vodka all by himself," the medic recounted with a chuckle.

Dr. Stone walked up and the medic withdrew a few steps.

"Private, are you certain that the water you drank from that pond yesterday was the only potential source of contamination you've been exposed to in the week or so since, uh, since we've been here?"

Matt thought back over the week. He had been assigned to find sources of water, along with several other men. They had found, marked on a map, and gathered samples from at least a dozen different locations, but he hadn't drunk from any of them... until yesterday.

"Yes sir... Doctor. We've been bringing you those samples following the procedure you told us. I haven't drunk from any of them, except for yesterday," Murphy replied, feeling like a child that just broke his mom's vase playing ball in the house.

The doctor looked down at him, "And what may I ask changed yesterday?"

Matt had been dreading this part of the conversation. "We were, uh, sort of playing a game."

"This should be good, elaborate Private," the doctor ordered.

"Several of us guys, we'd been collecting this stuff all week you know. And we started challenging each other, kind of daring each other, to take sips," Matt said. "A couple days ago different guys stepped up and took a drink, so that put the pressure on the others. Then yesterday, it kind of came to me and I didn't want to let the guys down."

Dr. Stone said, "Oh yes, I'm quite familiar with the psychology of a young man needing to prove that he does indeed have testicles. In fact they are often larger than his brain it seems."

"It was just a tiny sip, I practically just inhaled it," Matt tried to defend himself, knowing it was pathetic.

"Yes, how could a microscopic little organism cause any trouble? You are familiar with human reproduction yes? Sperm are microscopic, but just look at all the trouble one of those can cause," the doctor lectured. "It would be funny except that we don't need a bunch of you fellows all getting sick and using up medicine and other supplies needlessly that we can't replace. I'm sure we'll have plenty of real problems to face without creating our own."

"I'm sorry sir. I'll make sure and tell the other guys to stop," Matt said.

"Don't bother, I'll take care of them," the doctor said, then his voice softened.

"I think you may have legionellosis, which is potentially fatal. Now, the good news is I don't think you have the more serious form, which is called Legionnaires' disease, because you've become sick too quickly. Not intuitive is it?" the doctor asked.

Matt shook his head.

"Since you came down with symptoms so quickly, and because you are otherwise a healthy young man, it indicates to me that you likely have the much milder Pontiac fever," Dr. Stone concluded.

"What?"

"Most people haven't heard of it but trust me, it's real. I want to keep an eye on you and treat you with an antibiotic that is very effective against the more serious of the two as a precaution as it can be fatal if not treated early. Just in case you forgot sticking your head in a swamp four days ago," the doctor said, his condescending tone returning briefly.

"I think you'll be fine Private," the doctor reassured and then walked away.

Matt just lay on the cot, grimacing with the pain, and hoping he'd be able to sleep through the worst of it.

* * *

Dr. Stone returned to his desk after attending to Private Murphy thinking to himself, *I guess I won't be inviting Private Murphy and his cohorts to join me once I'm ready to leave... then again, dumb underlings don't ask as many questions.*

Damon went back to looking at the map he'd been making all his research notes on over the past few days. One last trip the previous evening had completed the data gathering portion of the project. Now it was on to calculation.

By carefully digging in the valley he had been able to uncover the boundary of the measurable effects of the event. Anywhere he dug that had a second layer of grass a foot or two below the top turf had been *imported* during the time travel incident. If there wasn't grass below, it meant that the area didn't contain any matter from the 21st Century.

The dissected tank gun barrel had demonstrated this beautifully, and easily. By estimating, approximating, and a whole lot of digging, the doctor had exposed three small pits that showed the actual line of transition where the sub layer of grass suddenly ended.

As he had expected, the shape was a broad arc across the valley. Then laying down a board with an inverted T shape on the boundary he had been able to determine the direction to the center of the phenomenon. He did this on each of the boundary points he had identified.

After that it was simple to connect the two most distant locations with a line to form the base of a triangle. In truth getting the line deployed had been difficult, but as long as the bearing to the opposing corner had been correct then his measurements would be as well.

It was simple geometry. The two points, roughly two hundred meters apart, pointed toward the center of the event, where Stone hoped to find... something. He also knew it might prove fruitless. But it was the most logical place to start.

Knowing the distance between the points, and the angle of each of these corners meant that, after applying some trigonometry, he could calculate the length of the sides of the triangle, and thus be able to find the center of the event.

In fine scientific fashion, Dr. Stone had recorded his measurements three separate times. He was presently plotting out the center based on the third set of numbers. While far from surgical, it did give him three possible locations for the center, all fairly close to each other. Within that set of points he would find... whatever was there was to be found.

Looking at the final plot and then accounting for where the vehicles of the unit were at present, he realized he'd have to be discreet with the next phase of his investigation. The three possible locations looked to be right here in the middle of Camp Nowhere. He wanted to have a chance to investigate solo prior to involving anyone else in the unit. Depending on what he found he might or might not share the knowledge...

Tomorrow he would have to head out to the village to begin working there as well. Stone knew that would slow down his research, but it was important to do. There were people that needed his skills. Also, it was time for him to start learning the language. After all the quick results of the past few days, it would be hard to slow down. But it wasn't a race because no one else was thinking along these lines, he smiled to himself.

Patience.

Chapter 14: Two Weeks Later

Lieutenant Pontus woke up and crawled out from inside the crude wood shelter he had slept in. It was low to the ground, it leaked and didn't have any of the touches of home but he was only ever there to sleep. He emerged glad to see the sun after two weeks of mostly rain. All around him wisps of fog were steaming up from the ground.

John rubbed a hand across his face feeling the stubble. He had been slacking on some of the finer details because they didn't seem to matter here. Being around the villagers everyday he had grown accustomed to a more natural earthy look.

John looked around and saw a few other men crawling out of the little buildings, each of which could hold up to four people, the collection of which the men called Shanty Town.

"Good morning lieutenant," one of the men said.

Pontus acknowledged him with a nod, "We going to get that framework done today?"

"Well sir, if we do that, what would we do tomorrow?" the young man joked.

The group had been chosen based on skills, those with construction background were especially valuable. John had been impressed with what these guys had been able to accomplish, they knew their way around a wood shop. They were building framing using timber they had cut down by axe and shaped with other tools, some of which were improvised. The current project was building a clinic for the doctor to see patients and to serve as his quarters when in the village. He had turned up his nose at Shanty Town.

The colonel had decided that the unit would adopt the village more or less, providing them assistance in hopes of continuing to befriend them and learning more about them and from them. So in addition to the clinic, the construction team had been through every building in the village looking for problems that needed to be repaired, walls that were on the verge of collapse, roofs that leaked.

John was okay with this assignment, he liked to help, and seeing the smiles from the locals, especially the children, made him feel genuinely happy for the first time since their arrival here.

John put on an army issued green t-shirt and camo pants and then a straw colored tunic that he got in the village. He had found it surprisingly effective in repelling the sun. It also helped him to blend in, a difficult task given that he was six inches taller than any of the villagers. Lastly, he picked up his Beretta M9 pistol and belt, which he worked under the robe.

Lieutenant Pontus walked downhill to the path and waited for the rest of the men to join him. Once there he stopped and took in the natural beauty of the valley. Spring was in full bloom now and everywhere was green and the river was running swiftly.

He heard soft footsteps behind him and turned to see three women walking down the trail toward him, carrying jars of water. He had seen the tall young woman only a few times in the past two weeks. He learned that her name was Meishan, and he always smiled to her, well he smiled at *all* of the villagers. Here she was coming down the trail, last in the line. He waited for the other two to pass, smiling at each, and then when it came to Meishan he said "Hello" to her in her own language.

She returned the smile, a touch of surprise in her eyes and replied to him but he didn't understand what she said.

Maybe she said "good morning" he thought as she passed by heading toward the village.

His thoughts were interrupted as the other men came down and joined him on the trail. Together they headed to the village. In just a few minutes, John and the group arrived at the clinic build site located on the far, north, side of the village. He saw that Cong had beaten them there, as he did every day.

John had befriended Cong, the first man they had met in the village. Cong started teaching John the local language, which his fellow soldiers called Old Korean, or just "Okor." John didn't want to have to depend on the interpreters that were being trained. He also didn't understand why the colonel hadn't instructed everyone to start learning the language. This was their world now, anyone they came into contact with outside the village might speak Okor or something similar, but certainly not English.

The clinic site was close to the village main entrance which was demarked by a low fence stretching from the base of the nearby slope on the left down toward the river on the right. In the middle was a gap roughly five meters wide, essentially an open gate. Beyond the gate there was a wide path, mostly overgrown, a rarely used road according to Cong. Lt. Pontus had walked it for a couple kilometers one day, there wasn't a lot to see just more of the same vegetation. He had wanted to explore it further but there was too much else to do.

"Hello," John said to Cong in Okor.

"Hello friend," Cong replied.

"What word for sun up?" John tried to ask.

Cong looked to the low sun and said a phrase that John repeated back, hoping it meant good morning.

Cong said, "Work, we work," pointing to the clinic.

"Yes, yes, work," John had come to learn that Cong was a task master.

By noon, the day had grown hot. John had worked up a sweat moving logs and helping to shape the ends of them with a sledge hammer and wedge. He removed his villager robe and took a break for water, downing it with big gulps.

Out toward the river he saw several women washing clothes and clay pots. He realized that the closest one to him was Meishan, and she appeared to be looking at him. Then she looked down at what she was doing. *Was she watching me?* he wondered.

He drank more water and then looked over at her. Again she was looking at him, and this time she didn't break eye contact right away. Instead, she gave a slight smile before continuing her work. John turned and went back to his task.

He was still trying to come to grips with life in this ancient world and there was so much work to be done. Now his mind was distracted thinking about this woman. The situation seemed complicated.

He realized then that he hadn't thought as much about his girlfriend Kathryn over the last several days. That first week he had thought of her frequently, wondering what she thought had happened to him, but also trying to accept that he would never see her again. If he were a prisoner of war he could comfort himself with the hope that he might eventually see her one day, but this wasn't the case. He had resigned himself to it, and so had started to suppress all thoughts of his former life as they just brought pain.

This was his world, this was his life, and he hoped that most of it was yet to be lived. He paused and looked over his shoulder at Meishan who was focused on her task.

Maybe it's not so complicated.

Chapter 15: Withdrawal

The journal, her way of compartmentalizing and analyzing herself, lay in the corner where she had thrown it days before. Renee was curled up on her bunk looking outside through the plastic mesh window of her shelter feeling hopeless.

Three weeks of this quiet torture, that was all it had taken to push her to madness, into her depths. No noise, no booze, no music, no bright lights or shopping, only... *nothing*. And that is what she felt like, a nothing.

After all these years, all she could see was the past, her last year of high school, staring back at her. She was a woman now, why was it that this is where her restless mind dwelled? She knew, but tried to rationalize it away, looking for an alternate meaning, something beyond the shattered end to her childhood, as her mother and father, once her foundation, had been turned into a crevasse by their divergent lives.

Twelve years gone by, and she was right back in the same place she'd been then, confronting the same awful reality that she'd never really accepted. One she'd merely hid from with activities and people, hard work and harder play. After more than a decade she was just a girl that missed her daddy, the new permanence of the separation finally sinking in. Renee wiped away yet more silently flowing streams from her face.

Anger at her mother flared up. *Why did you make me choose! Why did you take him away from me!*

Like the end of most marriages and relationships it had taken both her mom and dad. Or rather the continuation of the marriage would have taken effort from both of them, and she surmised that they had simply grown tired of the effort for whatever reason.

The final straw, whether it had been money or time away or... the other issues escaped Renee at this moment of grief revisited. The real reason had been simple, they had stopped trying, stopped putting the other one first. They'd sought after happiness in the form of one distraction or another.

Renee snickered at herself, *I'm so like them, chasing happiness that had once come simply by being alive.*

The rain outside was letting up, but the blackness persisted. It suited her mood, and she wrapped it around herself, absorbing the chill power of the darkness, being one with it.

The haunting and powerful vocals of Amy Lee crept into her consciousness,

Now I will tell you what I've done for you, 50 thousand tears I've cried.

At 17, when things had started to grow dim, her first solace had been dark music, it had served to stabilize the pain in her heart somehow.

Don't want your hand this time, I'll save myself.

The prickly image she had projected, quite successfully, was the opposite of what she had really wanted and needed.

I'm falling forever...

I've got to break through...

I'm going under...

Renee cried harder.

Before the darkness had completely consumed her she'd left for college. Free from seeing anyone who knew her, especially close friends and family, she'd been able to let go of the dark façade which wasn't much fun to be or be around. Instead she embraced a bright and happy one that was the life of the party.

This new escape was more sustainable and more socially acceptable. What's more, she was really good at it. She was friends with everyone, but no one knew her.

But there was no escape here in the mountains of Korea... save the ultimate one.

71

The officers had tried to keep it quiet, but it was common knowledge that there had been a suicide two nights before. A young private had left a note about missing his wife and kids and had slashed his wrist while alone in his tent.

Renee dwelled on the thought. She didn't want to die but just wanted the pain to stop.

God... why won't the pain go away?

Renee continued sobbing and held her rolled up blanket, clutching it like a teddy bear, wishing it would hug her back. Soon she drifted off to sleep and stayed asleep all the way till morning. It was her first full night's sleep in almost three weeks.

Chapter 16: The Date

After another week of hard work, and thankfully no more rain, the clinic was done. *Well, mostly* John thought. It was framed and the dissected tent panels had been stretched out over the frame and attached. The villagers were still working on the outer layer which would match the rest of the village and John's team was going to start assisting them with that chore.

Over the modular plastic floor, also liberated from camp, had been lain sheets of plastic to make it easier to clean and thus enable some level of sterilization. There was even some furniture brought from the main camp. A working desk, tables, chairs, bunks, a cabinet and even a field operating table.

Lieutenant Pontus stood back looking at the structure. *Not bad.* It had only taken them a few weeks to get it to this point. It was time to think more about the other projects they wanted to accomplish in the village over the next few months of good weather.

As he was thinking, he heard someone walk up on his left, so he turned to face... Meishan who stood smiling warmly. He noticed that her dark hair was glossy and her clothes were different than what he had seen her wear before. It was still a robe style outfit but it was closer fitting and made of a thinner material that was possibly silk, it was pretty.

She said, "Hello, Juh-n" in *English*.

John was shocked to hear this come out of her mouth. He smiled back, "Hello." Then he had his own surprise for her, "You look beautiful," he said in her language. He had been practicing it for days though it seemed a bit sophomoric.

She dipped her chin humbly and John wondered if she would blush. Then she looked up and her eyes bored deeply into his with sudden intensity and feeling. There was a depth to her that he couldn't explain, it wasn't based on knowledge, but rather intuition.

After a moment she spoke, this time in her language. He could barely make out a word, and couldn't catch her meaning. She motioned for him to come with her and was pointing toward some destination in the village. Then he heard her mention eating or food. She turned to go and motioned for him to follow.

John looked down at himself, he was dusty, sweaty, and hadn't shaved in days. *Oh well.* He nodded to her and said, "Yes," in her language.

Meishan gave a nod and began walking toward the center of the village. He caught up and walked beside her. Besides being clean, her hair looked different than he had seen it before. It was straight down the back of her head with an ornate headband holding it back and out of her face. He couldn't recall seeing any of the women, or men, wearing jewelry or decoration of any kind in his time with them.

* * *

Lang was 16 years old and therefore a man. Like all men of his village he worked at many different tasks depending on the needs of the day. This day it was removing weeds from the millet fields with tools and bare hands.

There were too few men in the village and it had been that way for as long as Lang could remember. Just a few years earlier there had been more, including his cousin Piao that he had looked up to like a big brother.

Of course, he also knew why they were gone. The older men and the women of the village rarely spoke of it, but he had heard enough over the years to know it was a recurring event. When the last group of men had left Lang remembered his mother had been terrified and held on to him, as if he might willingly run off to join them.

They had left behind much work, and Lang had grown up quickly after that. Working in the fields, constructing buildings, tending to the animals, hunting. Anything that the other men had done, Lang had done.

Besides friends, family and work, the young men had left behind something else, girls. Girls that had no one to become their mates. Two of them were his sisters, Jin and Yin. He was sad for them, but after the initial pain of loss they seemed to move on well. They too worked and served in the village. There was little time to mourn with so much to do to survive.

Lang's departed cousin was supposed to be joined to the third girl that had become a woman during this time, Meishan.

He had known Meishan all of his life. As a young boy he had liked her because she would take the time to play with him, even when his twin sisters did not. As he got older, things changed and she began to make him nervous. Meishan was beautiful in form and pleasant in behavior, but he didn't understand why he felt sick whenever he was around her.

"You know you are becoming a man," his cousin had said, "when your body grows stronger but girls make you weaker."

Over the past few months, it seemed that his dream might finally come to be. His mother and aunt had been talking with Meishan's mother. After much discussion it was decided that, come the dry season, they were to be joined together.

But then, almost a complete moon ago, the green men had come. Village life, unchanging year after year, was suddenly upset with the arrival of these big men who wore strange clothing and came mostly in pale white and dark brown skin.

Lang had been there to see their arrival. At first there was apprehension throughout the whole village, and he had readied his sword, determined not to be taken without a struggle. But then the visitors had amazed everyone with strange objects and incredible tools, made of a metal he had never seen before. He too had been taken in, awed by them.

But as he had seen more and more of them he had decided.

They aren't better than me.

He had seen them working, and they struggled with effort, sweated and grew tired, just as he did. Their tools were a wonder, but he had been given one of their axes to use for a time, and once he adjusted to its odd shape, he had worked just as quickly as they.

Lang stopped his work in the field. He laid down his tool and stretched his arms up and behind his head, there he felt the handle of the sword which he always kept strapped to his back.

Looking across the field back toward the village he saw the green men at work on the new building, a place for their healer to work. The healer, *he* was worthy of much respect and gratitude. He could make injuries whole again, removing pain and corrupt flesh by way of some kind of magic. Truly he must be an agent of the gods and Lang always treated him with reverence.

Lang saw one of their leaders standing near the building. His name was John. John had been friendly to him at that first meeting. But when Lang had asked to see the man's sling, he had denied him. Besides the slings that all of the green men wore, he had seen them carry no other weapons besides the axes and large knives, no long swords, no spears, no bows.

Lang had counted himself and the village blessed to have these strangers come to them. Until yesterday...

He had been eating the evening meal with the others in his family. His sisters were carrying on as usual laughing and whispering things to each other. Then they grew quieter and actually looked sad and they kept glancing over at him. Having two older sisters, he was accustomed to such behavior and just ignored them.

Later that night his sister Jin pulled him outside to talk.

"Brother, things are happening and I want you to know of them."

"Our mother talked with Meishan's mother yesterday," she said with quiet intensity. "She is asking to delay your union with Meishan for a time."

The news had struck Lang's heart like a spear, "Why? She is your closest friend, why is this?"

Jin looked away before speaking, "She has not spoken of this to us, I was as surprised as you to hear this. I think that this is her mother's doing."

He struggled to respond, his voice tightening, "There is something you are not saying."

She looked back to his eyes, "Meishan has been talking of the newcomers a great deal. In particular that tall one that has been working in the village."

Now as he watched John walking with Meishan an anger burned.

He is not better than me.

* * *

John wasn't sure what to say. He only knew a little of her language and most of it was practical communication stuff, not conversational. He tried, "The sun is nice."

She turned to look up at him as they walked and he thought she said, "Warm is nice."

There it was their first conversation, and it was about the weather…

"John, leader," she said in broken English. He wasn't sure if it was a statement or a question.

"Yes I'm a leader, an officer," he replied. Then in her language, "Yes."

Meishan turned to a home in the middle of camp. John was suddenly aware that several people were watching, including one of his soldiers. He smiled to them and followed as she entered the shack of a house.

Once inside, he saw that there was a meal prepared and laid out on the floor on top of a straw matt. An older woman greeted them, saying something that John didn't understand but which was delivered with a pleasant smile.

Meishan said, "Ping," as she reached out to place her hand on the woman's shoulder. It wasn't hard to guess that this was her mother, but was "Ping" her name or did "ping" mean mother?

Ping wasn't tall like Meishan, and her facial features were round and soft. But in her eyes he saw the same intensity that at once reminded him of Meishan.

Oh boy. John thought then said in English, "A pleasure to meet you," reaching out a hand to her. The villagers didn't have a handshake in their culture, though they had been catching on and it didn't seem to bother them. In return she patted his outstretched arm and gestured for him to sit.

They all sat and began eating the meal. The food was tastier than anything John had sampled before during his time in the village. There was fish or meat mixed into each dish. Trying to have good manners he had to use restraint not to stuff himself.

Dinner was mostly quiet. Meishan and her mother would occasionally exchange words and looks with each other. They also directed questions or comments at John from time to time that he couldn't understand. The conversation wasn't particularly productive.

As the dinner was winding down, her mother started talking quite a lot. She gestured at Meishan and then at John, she was trying to get some message across. Then she stood and motioned for the two of them to stand as well. She took one of each of their hands and then brought them together so that they clasped. Meishan's hand was rough but warm, and her fingers were long and slender.

Then her mother motioned that they should go outside as she rambled on, saying what, John did not know. But he got the general idea.

I guess we're on a date, he thought.

Outside the sky was mostly dark now, there was just a thin arc of azure on the western horizon. Above them, the sky was midnight blue and sparkling with stars. They walked in between a few dwellings into the clear meadow then the path that led to the village water collection point.

Her left hand was in his right as they walked slowly on the path. John wished he could talk to her, find out what she liked, what she disliked. He looked at her and she turned to him smiling warmly. She gave his hand a light squeeze that conveyed that she valued him, like he was filling a need.

Looking up he had a thought. There was one phrase he had learned well. He stopped and pointed to the nearly full-moon in the sky.

"What is the name for that?"

She looked up at it, then pointed as well, and replied with a word, "Yue."

"Yue," he repeated. She corrected him slightly and he said it again.

He turned to her, then placing his hand on his chest he stated in her language, "like moon," not remembering how to refer to himself in her speech.

"*I* like moon," she replied teaching him.

Then she said something else that John didn't understand, but she seemed to be talking about the moon, perhaps why she liked it. Whatever it was, by the way she talked and gestured, it was clearly something she had given some thought.

Her face was soft in the moonlight. John wasn't sure what the customs were in this culture and didn't want to offend or insult her but in that moment he was taken with her and felt compelled to reach out and touch her smooth cheek, but he resisted.

Though they couldn't talk, his attraction to her was more than just her outward beauty. As they looked into each other's eyes he felt a connection to her. It was like they were at the same place, on the same page. Her eyes and face were devoid of guile. She wasn't holding anything back, this was rare to find in the world he had come from.

For another hour, they just wandered back and forth on the trail, mostly in silence sharing looks and smiles. John would have never guessed that these would be the main ingredients for a great first date.

Chapter 17: The Skirmish

Lieutenant Pontus and Sergeant Turner were collecting leftover material and tools from the build site. There were still a few odds and ends to do before the clinic was completely finished, but it was functional. It was midday and John was thankful that the temperature was not as warm as it had been the previous week.

John reflected again on the time he'd spent with Meishan the previous night. He hadn't stopped thinking about her.

A sound interrupted John's thoughts. It was a distant drumming but getting louder quickly. He looked around trying to determine its direction and source.

Sergeant Turner said, "Sounds like horses Lieutenant."

John hadn't seen any horses in the village, but agreed that it did sound like several horses at a gallop. He looked past the entrance of the village and down the road. About 200 meters away he saw horses with riders.

Lieutenant Pontus tugged on the sergeant's robe and they moved back around the corner of the clinic but continued to watch the approaching horsemen. As they got closer, he could make out five individuals wearing dark clothing.

He heard concerned shouts from some of the villagers. John couldn't see back into the rest of the village from his position but he could hear some villagers coming closer apparently to meet the riders.

Once the men closed to within 50 meters they slowed their mounts. It was then Pontus could see that four of the men were holding bows in one hand. As they came to the fence that was the threshold of the village all of them came to a stop and these four produced arrows, readying their bows, but did not draw them.

John could see they were wearing crudely fashioned armor, he guessed it was tanned leather and was covered sporadically with small metal plates. They weren't identical but the similarity had the same effect, they were uniforms. Their left arms were covered in armor, but the right arm of each man was exposed below the shoulder.

Pontus saw the village leaders Kuson and Cong moving forward to meet the riders, they appeared nervous. Only a few other villagers were present, mostly older women.

The lead rider, the only one not brandishing a bow, stepped off of his modest sized horse. He strode confidently into the village and approached Kuson. He spoke clearly, with authority, but wasn't shouting nor did he appear angry. It sounded like he was asking, or demanding, something of the leader. He was speaking the same language as the villagers. He thought he heard the word for "man" used once or twice.

The leader responded by shaking his head and opening his hands, saying something in a submissive tone.

The intruder's calm demeanor vanished in an instant as he shouted and grabbed Kuson by his shoulders then gestured at the rest of the village. Then he pointed at some of the women and said something else.

John noticed Cong bristle at this but he made no move to interfere. Kuson spoke emphatically in a begging tone.

Lt. Pontus was growing increasingly nervous, he didn't like the direction this was heading. The colonel hadn't discussed this scenario with his officers, an oversight in retrospect.

It was hard to intervene in an argument when you didn't know the first thing about what was being argued over. He didn't know who these warriors belonged to but clearly they were part of a larger organization. They were threatening a defenseless people and demanding something unknown to him. People that he and the rest of the unit had formed a friendship with.

His decision was made.

"Sergeant," he whispered as he drew his M9 pistol from its holster, holding it down at his side. The sergeant followed the lieutenant's lead drawing his 9mm handgun as well.

The distance was about 20 meters, a tad long for precision with a combat handgun, but well within effective range. John hoped that it wasn't going to come to that but that thought evaporated as he saw the intruder draw a small sword.

"I've got the leader, you start from the right," he said calmly to Sergeant Turner.

Lt. Pontus took careful aim at the man's back and fired a shot, followed by two more. Sergeant Turner moved out from behind the lieutenant and opened up on the first mounted archer on the right, firing rapidly.

Pontus saw his target flinch from the impact of at least one of the rounds and he shifted aim to the first mounted archer on the left. The bowmen were wide eyed and their horses began to whinny and buck, making hitting the riders more difficult. John just kept adjusting his aim and squeezed off round after round.

One rider had fallen off of his mount and another was leaning to one side. A third was gaining control of his horse and turning it around to flee. The lieutenant couldn't see the fourth.

Pontus and the sergeant both stopped firing. Though his ears were ringing from the gunfire, he could hear voices shouting and screaming.

Cong and Kuson were crouched behind a nearby pile of wood with a terrified look. The other villagers that had been around had retreated inside buildings. All except one young man who held a sword and looked on mouth agape.

The lieutenant and sergeant approached the enemy leader who was face down on the ground but still clutching his sword in one hand. It looked like he had been hit twice, once in the middle of his back and once in the leg.

Lieutenant Pontus holstered his pistol and took the sword from the man's hand. Leaving him there he and Turner approached

83

the spooked horses and their riders. One man had fled on his mount, John could see him about 100 meters away at full gallop. He came across a second warrior who was on the ground and wasn't moving. John could see blood on the man's face. A third man was obviously wounded, leaning over his horse's neck, making no attempt to fight.

Where are you number four? John thought.

He saw another horse with no rider a few meters away, it was bleeding from a gunshot wound to the shoulder. Sergeant Turner led the way toward the horse with his pistol. They approached cautiously but the horse dashed off a ways. They looked around in the tall grass, trying to find the fourth bowman. Finally they saw long black tangled hair, the man was face down in the grass, hands on his head with no obvious injury.

John couldn't think of a better word in his limited local vocabulary so he said, "Hello!" sternly as he stood above the man with sword poised to strike if necessary.

The man turned to look up at them, fear contorting his face. He mumbled something then buried his head again.

By this time a few villagers had ventured forward looking at the fallen warriors. The young man with a sword came up to John and bowed his face, said something, then looked up at John and spoke what sounded like a question.

John had no idea what the boy was going on about, so he just patted him on the shoulder and said, "It's okay, you're okay," before moving off to take a look at the wounded rider who still sat atop his horse.

Soon several other soldiers arrived, pistols drawn to see what had happened. In the end, there were one dead, two wounded and one unharmed but scared out of his mind. The fifth rider had fled back the way they had come.

It had taken a month, but the soldiers of the 4th Armored Cavalry Regiment had finally made their mark on history.

* * *

Lang heard commotion outside. It was rare that anyone came to the small village that was his lifelong home. And the only times there had been shouting such as this was when *they* had come before, servants of Warlord Zhu.

Lang ran out of his home crossing to the buildings on the other side of the village. This gave him a concealed approach to the front of the village. Heart pounding he drew his sword as he reached the last dwelling, then cautiously peeked around the corner to see five of Zhu's warriors.

Every few turns of the seasons the riders would come to gather young men from the village, taking them away and making them serve the warlord. There was never any word of what became of them after that, only memories and sadness for friends and family. Lang's father had been taken away when he was just a small child, he had only a faint memory of him.

Lang saw Kuson talking with the invader. He knew that the village elder was a strong man and could fight if needed, but also that to resist them would mean sure destruction for the village as the warlord's warriors would surely seek revenge.

Lang knew they were here to take him. He was now of the proper age and strength to be useful to them. He had no intention of submitting however. It wasn't such a far distance to cover to thrust his sword into the black clad intruder. The only question was whether he could get there before the archers' arrows pierced him.

Out of the corner of his eye, Lang saw two of the green men, including John, coming around the corner of the new building across from him. He glanced back when he heard shouting from the warrior who drew his sword. His heart raced as he prepared to charge.

Crack! Crack! Crack!

The noise split through his head and echoed around him. Lang reached his freehand up to cover one ear. He looked back to John and the other man. The small black objects in their hands were spitting fire and smoke and continued emitting that ear piercing noise, which was like lightning and thunder.

Then Lang saw that the riders were falling to the ground, wounded by an unseen force. The thundering sound finally ceased and he saw John and the other man approaching.

Thunder Sling he thought. It was then that Lang realized with horror, *They must be gods!*

The young man recalled all the anger and hatred he had felt at John, in an instant it was transformed into guilt and fear. The newcomers had just struck down five warriors with only a token effort on their part. Of course Meishan was to be his. He must have chosen to take her as his own, and how could she resist this being? What if John knew of his anger, what would he do?

Lang knew when to be humble, he had learned from village leaders, and he immediately went forward to speak to John. As he walked by the first fallen warrior he saw the bloody hole in his back.

They hurl stones with such force that they sink in like arrowheads! he thought amazed.

He caught up to John and stepped next to him, bowing he said, "Please forgive me, I did not know of your power and authority." Then looking up he asked, "Will you allow me to serve you?"

John reached his hand out, and Lang was momentarily fearful, but he only touched him on the shoulder and said something in a reassuring tone before turning and moving off.

It was then Lang realized that he wasn't going to be taken away as a captive or die this day. John had saved him from this fate, and had protected the whole village. Lang would serve him to the death if needed.

Lang ran to find his mother and sisters to tell them all that had happened.

Chapter 18: Aftermath

Colonel Erickson stood looking down at the bodies of three dead men.

He had just listened to Lieutenant Pontus and Sergeant Turner recount the details of the one-sided skirmish that happened earlier in the day. Not having given any direction about this kind of encounter it was hard to fault the young lieutenant's honor and sense of duty. It had been the right thing to do, even if it did complicate their lives.

"A had one of our men take a horse and scout down the road a ways. He came across the fifth man and his horse. The guy was on the ground already dead. He was able to put him on the horse and bring him back here," Lieutenant Pontus said pointing to one of the three bodies.

Erickson just nodded, taking it in.

"Colonel," Pontus resumed, "I wanted to make sure you saw the marks they have on their right forearm."

Lt. Pontus squatted down and with a pen pointed out the details as he spoke, "Looks like a snake or a serpent."

Erickson leaned down to get a closer look at the design's small wedge shaped head and wavy body, it reminded him of a classic picture of a sea serpent. Then he asked, "Is that branded into their skin?"

The lieutenant replied, "I believe so sir, just like a cow. But it also looks like something was added to give it that black color, looks a bit like a tattoo in that regard."

The colonel winced as he considered the pain involved in applying such a mark onto a person. He mulled the design over briefly. "Must be a sign of their army or their leader."

Colonel Erickson stood up and walked slowly away from the dead men, with Pontus following next to him.

"They'll send someone to look for them," the colonel said matter-of-factly.

The lieutenant was nodding, "Yes, sir."

The colonel mulled it over for a minute. "Probably send a substantially larger force. They will think that at best they were ambushed by the village, or at worst encountered a rival group. Which, in effect they did."

The lieutenant responded, "From what I've been able to gather from our interpreters, they were here to conscript men from the village. Not for the first time. Also, I think the leader of this group is named Zhu, he's some kind of chief or warlord. Not sure how many people we are talking about, but a large number figure hundreds."

In retrospect Erickson was thinking it had been inevitable that something like this would happen. The world had always been ruled by force or threat of force. Even if he had tried to keep the unit isolated and secluded, they were bound to make contact with a hostile force eventually.

"Alright, let's get them buried," he said. "We need to prepare for whatever might come. Figure that we should have at least two days before they get around to investigating. Start working up a short term plan for the defense of this village Lieutenant. I'd like to hear it at 0900 tomorrow."

Lt. Pontus replied sharply, "Yes, sir."

Nearby, Dr. Stone walked out of the clinic with a scowl on his face. "Make it four dead Colonel. He had just lost too much blood."

The colonel nodded.

Pontus spoke, "Sir, that still leaves us with one prisoner. He's scared out of his mind, and as such will probably be cooperative, the villagers have him bound and under guard. He might be able to give us information on enemy numbers, if we can get the interpreters to talk to him."

The colonel nodded, "See to it."

* * *

As the sun was getting low, John decided there wasn't much further he could do to prepare until morning. As he let his mind rest, it immediately went to Meishan. After the attack he had briefly checked to make sure she was okay, but hadn't spoken to her.

Now he was driven to see her. He walked the familiar path through the huts coming to hers. He called through the door, "Meishan?"

In a moment her mother Ping opened the door, a smile on her face. She ushered him in and started talking. He couldn't understand what she was saying but it seemed like happy talk. As John listened, he noticed that unlike the other villagers he'd come into contact with that day, she wasn't looking at him with awe.

Meishan appeared from the back room, her face stoic. Ping took her daughter's hand pulling her into the room, saying something to her. Then she took John's hand and motioned for them to sit. John and Meishan both sat down on the mat used for eating their meals and then her mother went outside.

He said "Hello," in her language.

"Hello," she replied, but avoided eye contact.

John leaned down, trying to make her look at him. She eyed him, said something he didn't understand and then her eyes darted away.

This was so frustrating. Just two nights before they'd had dinner in her home and gone for a walk. A connection had started to form but now it was severed.

He wondered if she thought he was some kind of superior being. He tried to think of a way to show her that he wasn't. He reached out to hold her hand, she hesitated but then took it. He pulled it close and placed her palm on his chest. He hoped that she could feel his heartbeat. She looked at her hand on him and he thought she might pull it away.

"Man," he said softly in her language, "John."

She looked up but shook her head slightly.

John took her hand and intertwined his fingers with hers.

"Man, woman," he said.

She squeezed his hand then clasped her other hand around it as well. She looked up and John could see her eyes were moist. She said, "Man."

She gets it, he thought, he hoped.

Even before the firefight, many of the villagers looked at them as if they were some greater beings. But Meishan had seemed to understand better than most, she was respectful, but not subservient. Similar to how Kuson treated them.

She started crying then took his hand and pulled it up to her chest. He could feel her heart beating rapidly beneath the coarse material of her shirt. They sat in silence for a time.

Gradually her tears ceased and her countenance shifted to the one he recognized. She loosened her grip on his hand and lowered it.

"I like moon," he said to her in Okor.

She stifled a laugh, "I like moon," she replied.

Then she relaxed and smiled at him. Now John could finally relax too. He had almost lost her, but now the connection was back.

Chapter 19: Preparations

Colonel Erickson woke with the sun coming in a window of the clinic where he lay on a mat. He had decided to spend the past two nights in the village rather than hike back to Camp Nowhere and then come back each morning. Getting up he poked his head into the doctor's office and saw that he wasn't in his bed.

Erickson really wanted coffee and some breakfast. However, he knew he was likely to find only bread and water in this village, and he would make do and be thankful for it. William Erickson had spent his entire adult life in the army, and had learned early on to eat what you could when it was available.

Outside Erickson felt a chill in the air. Someone in the unit had determined that it was May. That same person was trying to identify the exact date but said that would have to wait for the summer solstice.

The colonel saw several villagers near one of the fire pits a short distance away. He decided to be sociable and walked over, smiling to the small crowd of mostly women. As he arrived there was an air of wariness in the group, something he hadn't sensed from the villagers before, not even at the first meeting.

Of course. He realized it was because of the shooting two days before. *They must think we are using magic of some kind.* He decided their caution was understandable. Erickson backed away slowly, still smiling. He'd have to talk to Kuson to have him explain to the people that they shouldn't fear his men.

Turning away he saw Dr. Stone coming out of the only large building the villagers had before the clinic it was a meeting hall. The doctor saw him right away.

"Colonel, I was just coming to see you. I think you had better come take a look at something," the doctor said.

As Erickson walked over to the doctor he got an uneasy feeling. He followed the doctor into the building where a gas lantern was adding to what little sunlight filtered into the large room.

Before him was a man, bound to a chair, wearing peasant clothes with blood poured out all down the front of his body and pooled below him. His head was lolled to one side and his neck had been cut dramatically.

"The prisoner," he stated.

"Yes sir, the prisoner. One of the young lads came and pulled me out of bed urgently. I assumed it was a medical emergency with a villager, I didn't know it involved the prisoner or I would have roused you as well," the doctor said.

"Of course Doctor, tell me what you've been able to learn."

"I estimate he's been dead for no less than two hours, no more than four," Dr. Stone began. "His neck was cut with a sharp but crude blade, not a surgical knife and not one of the combat knives that we and some of the villagers now have."

The colonel thought a moment and said, "Probably one of the villagers getting revenge for past actions by this warrior group or perhaps even this very man."

The doctor nodded but said nothing.

"I would be mad, but this is their business. We were here to help, but they wanted to guard him, which I supported. Kuson will have to decide how it happened, if he cares, and if he wants to punish someone or not," the colonel said.

Then he added, "As long as it wasn't one of our guys. Any reason to think it was?"

"No sir, I can't think of anyone that would have motive. These people have done nothing against us. The murder of the prisoner seems personal, passionate. Someone with an axe to grind, oh, pardon my choice of words," the doctor winced.

"Alright, let's go talk to Kuson," the colonel said.

*   *   *

Lieutenant Pontus wanted to see how things were progressing on the defenses being built around the village. After assessing the situation he'd know where to put additional resources and where to jump in and help himself.

As he walked through the middle of the village and got to the entrance he heard a voice sing out, "Lieutenant."

Then he saw Sergeant Kyle Turner approaching, "Yes Sergeant?"

"I think I've got those guys squared away on how we want the berm built up. It took me showing them for a while, but now they are moving good. They're no strangers to hard work," the sergeant said.

Pontus looked down past the village entrance. The tall grass and weeds had been cleared for a distance of 50 meters. The villagers and his men had made a lot of progress in just a day and a half. Pontus' plan was to have the grass cut out to 100 meters by the next day, which was on track. Eventually he wanted it cleared out to the full line of sight from the village, about 200 meters.

On the left side of the road, at the base of the slope, there was an earthen berm two feet high and as many thick. This too would be extended to a length of 100 meters and sooner was better because some of his men would need to work on it after that. He wanted all of the berm work completed by the next night.

"Very good, I'm going to head to the other side of the river to check on progress there," the lieutenant said.

Pontus started walking toward the river. As he reached the edge of the village he saw two soldiers with rifles slung and wearing full battle gear. They were two of the eight men posted as guards around the village, most of them near the entrance. They increased their bearing as he approached,

"Good morning Lieutenant," one of them called.

"Stay sharp men," he said firmly.

93

Next he walked across the narrow foot bridge over the river near the clothes washing area. Once on the other side he saw the four men that were working on building a machinegun emplacement. The site was on top of a slight mound, and built up further so that it would have about three meters of height above the river once completed. The base was dirt, with rough logs for walls, outside it was sandbagged. There were three openings, one facing the village, another the road and the third an open field to the east. These were the only practical axes of approach given the terrain.

Stacked just outside the wall of the pillbox were several cans of 7.62mm ammunition and an M240 machine gun.

"It's looking good men," he said approvingly.

"Thank you sir," came a reply from a man stacking bags.

Sergeant Paulson stood up to face the lieutenant, "You said you wanted it done quickly, so I've been focusing on an attack from the north, if someone gets in behind us, it won't do a hell of a lot a good."

The lieutenant nodded, "How about the roof?" Archers meant plunging fire was a concern. One of the villagers had demonstrated this the day before by launching several arrows from out on the road and landing a few right inside the bunker they were building. It was a useful demonstration of technology he and his men weren't accustomed to worrying about.

"The guys back at camp said they'd bring it out first thing tomorrow," the sergeant replied.

"Alright, keep things moving and by noon tomorrow keep a crew on the gun around the clock, and stay alert," the lieutenant instructed. "I'm heading up to check out the O-P now."

Lieutenant Pontus thought that the machine gun bunker would be plenty to stop even a moderate sized threat, as long as it was amply protected. But he didn't want to stop at the bare minimum. The most important factor in repelling an attack was knowing when it was going to come.

Pontus continued walking away from the village across the valley and hiked up the tree covered slope. It took him about 15 minutes to reach the plateau observation post (OP), which he saw was just a small clearing at the base of a tree overlooking the valley. Looking back the way he had come, he could see the village in the distance through breaks in the trees.

Lt. Chris Franks from the Headquarters anti-aircraft (AA) section greeted John with an outstretched hand, "Taking in the sights John?" Franks and Pontus had known each other for two years and got along well.

"Yeah just kicking the tires. How did you get picked for this duty?" Pontus said.

Lt. Franks smiled, "Yes, well of all the vehicle missions we have, I guess the colonel decided the anti-aircraft mission was the most superfluous, so that freed me and my men to *hike* out here and become spotters."

John chuckled. Until the last two days, all the supplies and men going back and forth from the village and the camp had been hand carried, with rare exceptions. The urgency of the present mission to increase defensive measures *had* loosed up the use of a truck for moving some equipment, ammo and other supplies, but the troopers still had to walk it.

Chris added, "Word has it that he's going to start cutting down on battery use as well, wants to save them for a rainy day."

"So do you have a backup plan on how to communicate down to us?" Pontus asked.

"Well, I figured we'd just start practicing our smoke signals," he replied with a wry smile.

Pontus asked, "So, what *do* you have going on here?"

Lt. Franks' expression changed, becoming more focused. "I've got six men here right now. Two are clearing brush and cutting down trees that are blocking our line of sight to the machine gun nest and some sections of the road," he said pointing.

"Two more men are setting up the O-P so it's nice and cozy. The other two are moving supplies up here," he paused. "And me, well I'm basically just sitting on my ass," the humor returned to his voice.

"Sounds good," John said. "Mind if I check out the view?" reaching for his binoculars.

"Sure thing," Chris said handing over the optics.

Pontus trained the binoculars down into the village, between the trees there were good sightlines. Then he aimed them down to the road and off to the north from there. "Looks like you should be able to see a good kilometer or more down the road."

Franks nodded, "Yeah, I'm going to have one of my guys walk out there with a flag so we can get a better idea of just how far it is, where the dead spots are and so forth. The sun hits all along the road pretty well. We're in pretty good shape now, but in another day or so we'll be at one-hundred percent," he said confidently.

"Sounds good, after that it will just be a waiting game to see if anyone shows up."

* * *

Private Murphy was standing post at the back of the village, the side nearest Shanty Town which was about 100 meters away. He was listening to a verbal sparring match between his buddy Dominic Jones and Nick Reynolds, another scout from their platoon and a Southerner like Dom.

"I do miss sports," Nick Reynolds said before taking a long drag on a cigarette. "I mean I don't watch baseball anymore anyway, but I did enjoy watching some road racing in the summer."

Jones wrinkled his nose up, "NASCAR? You watch that crap? How can anyone watch that stuff. Many you are a sorry sack."

Nick wrinkled his face in return. "No not that, sports cars man, it's much more interesting than watching guys turn left for a couple hours. My daddy likes the NASCAR though." Then his face turned thoughtful, "I wonder if the Colonel would let us do some Hummer racing?"

"I can't believe you'd even bring up a shitty idea like that. Even if it wasn't about the worst idea I eva heard, the Colonel likely kill ya sorry ass for suggesting we waste fuel like that Marl," Jones countered.

"Would you stop calling me that, I've told you I don't even like Marlboro," Nick said as he lit another cigarette. "Now football, that's a game. I love watching that. Roll Tide!" then with a hint of loss in his voice, "Well, I used to," he said then took another long drag on his Lucky Strike.

Dominic perked up, "Oh, maybe you ain't so dumb as I heard. Now you talkin. I played a little tailback in high school. Now that we could get going. We could get ourselves a couple teams together."

"Dom, I think they might send you to officer candidate school if you keep coming up with ideas like that," Nick responded snidely. Then more evenly, "You know, I think you might have something there."

Then he looked at Murphy, "Hey, you can be one of our cheerleaders! I think that would suit you well," then laughed at his joke.

Murphy had become accustomed to some ribbing because of his slight build since his first day in the Army and had learned to just let it slide off. He'd been picked on and teased some in his childhood, but among soldiers it was like a professional sport.

Dominic responded, "What? I know you didn't just get on my man. You going to take that Murph?" He placed his arm on Matt's shoulder, "This here is a stone cold killing machine, he's got Medal of Honor written all over him. I'd watch your back if I was you *Nick*."

Dom reached into Matt's uniform and pulled out a spare rifle magazine then walked it over to Nick holding it up for him to see the exposed rifle rounds. "Look here, Murphy's already got

97

names written on these bullets. I'm sure he'll get yours onto one too, if he can figure out how to fit 'dumbass-inbred-whitetrash' onto the head of that little slug."

Murphy and the other man nearby chuckled. Nick just smiled and nodded his head.

Dominic said, "Here Murph," then tossed the magazine back to Murphy who wasn't expecting it and dropped it on the ground.

Dom looked on with disbelief as the other soldiers burst out laughing.

Dom said, "Okay, you can be the water boy."

Murphy felt his face flush slightly as he leaned down to retrieve the magazine. It had fallen open side down and upon inspection he noticed loose dirt was in the opening.

He removed his helmet and kneeling slid all 30 of the bullets out of the magazine one by one letting them fall into his helmet.

Dom and the others had moved a short distance away and Murphy saw one of the young men from the village approaching slowly. He appeared curious about what Matt was doing. As he got closer the man said something that Matt couldn't understand. Matt responded with the only word he knew in the local language.

"Hello."

Murphy continued with his task, shaking the dirt out of the now empty magazine. He'd give it a thorough cleaning when he got back to camp. But for now just wanted to load it back up and tuck it away. He started loading the AA battery sized brass cartridges into the magazine.

The young man reached out slowly and seemed intent on picking one of the bullets up out of the helmet. Murphy didn't know if he should let him or not. They were completely safe to handle so he decided to go the friendly route and motioned for him to go ahead.

The villager lifted up one of the bullets and seemed mesmerized by it. Then Murphy realized that the kid probably had no idea what it did. He stood and slipped the rifle off of his shoulder.

Matt held the rifle, muzzle up, and removed the magazine that was already in it, showing the man that it held the bullets. Then putting the magazine back in he pointed the gun in a safe direction and did his best with hand gestures to convey that the bullets came out of the barrel.

The whole while the young man looked on with wonder and then it looked like something must have clicked in his mind as his face changed somewhat.

Matt was happy, he felt like he had done his part to keep up friendly communication with the villagers. He took the bullet back from the young man, who gave it up with reluctance, then returned to the task of loading the magazine. The young man looked on until the very last one was replaced and Murphy tucked it back into a pocket.

Matt didn't know what to say so again he said, "Hello" in Okor and walked back to join his buddies. As he did he noticed the boy just stood watching him intently.

Strange kid.

Chapter 20: Equine

Renee Carlisle looked at herself in a small mirror on the wall of her tent and gave herself a slight smile as she tied her still damp blonde hair into a pony tail. She'd gone to the trouble of taking a shower today. The primitive, and cold, shower didn't use drinking water, but was sufficiently popular that its use was rationed. Renee slipped on a pair of well-worn designer jeans, tank top and cropped dark green denim jacket, then went out to embrace the morning.

She felt... renewed. The best she had felt in weeks or longer.

Over the previous few days she'd grown accustom to the painful thoughts of her past and was gradually accepting them. There was still genuine pain there, but things weren't as bad as she had feared. Suppressing them for so long had distorted their magnitude.

Renee walked in the direction of the mess tent. The offerings there weren't too appealing, but she had to eat something. Of her vanities and vices, worrying about and struggling with her weight had thankfully not been one of them. Her recent forgoing of food, dictated by her mood, had served to trim her down a few pounds to freshmen-in-college weight but losing any more would mean losing her curves and that just wouldn't do. Besides, she was hungry.

Entering the tent she saw that, as usual, the "pickins were slim," as her father would have said. But she always smiled to the people working there and never voiced any complaints while in the mess hall. She saw how hard the men and women worked to get something edible ready twice a day, she couldn't imagine a harder job than that in this new world.

Some foods she really missed, especially in the morning. But if she couldn't have her "green-goddess" coffee, banana and toast then she'd settle for whatever was being served. Today looked like fish, something bread-like made from wild grains, and water... again.

Food in hand, she left the tent and almost immediately spotted Sal, who greeted Renee with a smile and called for her to come over and sit with her and three other women. Renee was walking towards them when a sound caught her ear, a sound that immediately made her happy.

Turning and looking... there! A short distance away were four horses. One of them was shaking its head snorting and neighing contentedly. Renee's mouth opened and she smiled unconsciously. Her feet began moving of their own accord and she quickly closed the distance.

As she got closer Renee could see there were two different breeds. All were about 12 or 13 hands high, around four feet at the withers, which was pretty short. The first two were slender with graceful lines and looked like true horses, though shorter than those she'd grown up with. The other two were stocky, definitely a pony breed, with shaggy coats.

Several soldiers were nearby having a discussion, but Renee tuned them out focusing on the animals in front of her. She set her breakfast assortment on the ground and then moved around to their heads. Talking sweetly she gave each one a rub on the forehead and a pat on the neck.

One of the shaggy types responded to her affections and pushed back against her hand. He was light tan, almost blond in color but with a dark mane. The top of his head was just about even with hers so they were eye to eye.

"Oh, you're just adorable aren't you," she fawned.

Renee was vaguely aware that someone was approaching.

"Good morning Ms. Carlisle," came a deep friendly voice.

She turned to see Lieutenant Colonel Brower. She recalled that he was second in command of the unit. The other officers described him as "All Army" whatever that meant. She had found him to be approachable and sincere.

"Good morning Lieutenant Colonel," she said, then remembered belatedly that proper etiquette was to address him as "colonel".

"You like the newest members of our unit I see," he reached out and gave the pony nearest him a scratch on the mane. Next to his big frame, they looked almost like foals. "You ride do you?"

"Not in a long time. But I grew up with horses," she explained. "We always had them on our property. I think I spent more time riding than walking between eight and eighteen. I love them."

She *did* love them, she couldn't believe it had been so long, and that she really had forgotten the simple joy of going for a ride in the evening summer sun.

"You heard about the altercation in the village a couple days ago?" he asked. She nodded and he continued, "Well, these horses are spoils of war I guess and we're glad to have them. Since we want to save our fuel, we intend to put these little guys to work moving supplies and equipment between here and the village."

Renee felt excitement rise within her, "I want to help. I mean I'd like to be a part of that. But you need to be careful not to overwork these ponies. And the terrain is pretty rough, they aren't mules." She bent down to look at their feet and saw that they had a leather boot of some kind wrapped around each hoof.

"I don't know anything about these antiquated horseshoes, but I'm glad to see they have something. But you can't put a big soldier on these ponies, their feet won't take all that weight and abuse, certainly not without a proper shoe to protect them," she lectured.

"Yes ma'am."

Renee continued to inspect the horses, looking at their teeth and coats. "One of them is missing a shoe. You'll need to see about making another before having anyone ride her."

It was then that Renee realized that the lieutenant colonel was laughing softly, mostly to himself. "What's so funny?" she asked.

* * *

Nearby Dr. Stone walked into the new medical supply tent, located in the middle of the valley of Camp Nowhere. It had been easy to convince Lieutenant Colonel Brower that he needed a second location within the camp so that he could have one area for patients and another for supplies, equipment and so forth. And he said that it should be at a spot that was isolated, hard to sneak into, and therefore easy to guard.

Even after plotting the epicenter of the event, it had taken several days of probing with a thin metal rod to find the subsurface location. The bad weather had helped soften the ground, but had also hampered his excursions. Stone knew that he wouldn't be able to locate the epicenter unless, as he predicted, there was a 'something' there to be found.

There had been some false positives as he struck more than one rock in his search. He'd had to take it slow so that he didn't raise suspicion. Finally he had hit something different and he'd known almost immediately. It was about two feet down, and as he probed around the location, he'd felt the same scraping sensation a foot away then a meter away in a wide area. It had been very exciting.

The doctor had established the extent of the object, it turned out to be circular and roughly eight or nine feet in diameter. He marked the location and extent of the object subtly and then lobbied for his medical supply shelter, to be placed right over top of it.

In the week since the large tent had been erected, he'd first had supplies moved in, and built a wall of sorts all around the location of the underground object. After that he'd begun digging, *slowly*.

He took the time to dig when he could, he felt a bit like a prisoner tunneling out of his cell, which only increased the excitement. He had to be cautious so that no one noticed his activity, and he had to dispose of the dirt on occasion, which he typically did at night.

In his first day of excavation, he'd soon gotten down to the level of the large round object. After removing dirt and grass, he'd come upon a ropy material that turned out to be camouflage netting. *Very exciting.* He cut that with a knife and soon had uncovered the edge of the circle and realized it was about four inches thick.

Here he had paused to examine it more closely. It had a laminated construction, metal, plastic, composite and perhaps ceramic each in its own stratum. *Very interesting.* He guessed it had been designed to shield the thermal signature of whatever was below.

The next day he'd uncovered a large section of the edge and found that the large disc was supported by thick metal beams, of which he could see two, that continued down into the ground. The structure was like the roof of an underground gazebo. The area under the roof was completely filled with dirt and thus began the slow, hard work.

Dr. Stone had been able to stack boxes right on top of the structure, giving it even better concealment should anyone come snooping. Because of the importance of his medical supplies, he'd requested and received a guard detail to watch the tent when he wasn't there.

Progress had been slowed of late. He'd had to make frequent visits to the village to observe the construction of the clinic, treat villagers and keep up his language lessons. He had to temper his excitement, he was anxious to complete his excavation. *Patience*, he had told himself.

The last chance he'd had to dig, he'd removed enough material to find where two of the beams holding the roof connected to a concrete wall, establishing that there was a gap of roughly three feet between the two. Now, more digging.

With his body focused on the manual labor, Damon's mind was free to roam.

Supplies are good. Weapons are going to be more difficult. Still need to grow my pool of assistants. The two guards seem to be a lock. That smart ass lieutenant is a likely one, but I have to proceed carefully. I should approach Ms. Carlisle. She seems distraught, a positive, but also depressed, a risk. It would be easier if she sought my assistance.

As he continued mulling over his plans, his shovel struck something that sounded different. The doctor repositioned his lantern and took a closer look. Something was there in the dirt, *is that a rock?* He moved some more dirt away to the left and right of it and looked again.

Now he could see a dirt caked ear and part of a soft green cap. He used his hands to carefully remove more dirt from around it and at last he could clearly see the side of a head and the top of a shoulder covered in a green uniform jacket. It was a man buried in the dirt.

Another few minutes of cautious work and the doctor saw that it was an Asian man, and his style of hat and uniform looked to be that of a North Korean soldier.

"Hmmm...what were you doing down here my friend?"

Chapter 21: Nice Night for a Walk

John Pontus couldn't believe that it had only been a month since their arrival in this world, it seemed more like six. The different pace of life, and the newness of it all, made each day stretch out like the Sunday afternoons of his childhood. Maybe that was why the progression of his relationship with Meishan hadn't seemed too fast.

First three days had come and gone with no more visitors to the village. Now another three days had gone by and he wondered if they would ever come looking for their five missing warriors.

The lieutenant reflected on the fact that this wasn't the 21st Century. There were no satellites or real-time communications of any kind beyond face to face. The written message delivered by horseback was as high tech as it got. He, and his men, had to remain patient and vigilant or else they could find themselves overwhelmed in a moment.

The air was cooling with the afternoon sun and Lt. Pontus walked back to Shanty Town to clean himself up. After a shave and a waist-up sponge bath he put on fresh clothes and began the short walk back into the village to see Meishan.

Something about their inability to talk made him focus more on the unspoken nature of her being, and he liked what he saw. She was so natural and genuine. She knew nothing of the culture he had left behind with its hectic pace and where everyone seemed to wear a mask built up by years of empty pursuits, pains and disappointments.

There were plenty of hardships in her world, but they were more real, more authentic, than the things he had worried about when growing up, things like school, friends, cars, and girls. She worried about having food to eat and if their shelter would protect them from the next storm.

Her problems and her life seemed more real now to him than the life he'd been taken away from. And what's more, thinking about her helped him to forget. Helped him to not even remember that he should be mourning his previous life.

Since their reconnection the week before, he hadn't seen much of her. They were both busy with work to do, but she always had a soft expression for him whenever their eyes met. Yesterday he had tracked her down to let her know he wanted to see her today.

Now at her door John called out, "Meishan." He had found that knocking on doors unsettled the villagers.

He didn't have to wait long for her to appear. She was wearing the same pretty dress she had previously, her sleek black hair again straight and back. Her eyes looked somehow different, but as bright and full of life as ever.

"Hello, John," she said in English with a thin smile. Her pronunciation of his name sounded natural now, no longer a foreign word to her.

"You look beautiful," he said in her language.

She looked at him, accepting his complement with a modest smile and said, "thank you," in her tongue.

Then he led her out and away from the village taking the footbridge over the river.

At first John hadn't been sure what to do on this date, but had come up with an idea. They didn't say much of anything on the walk, but would occasionally share a glance or a gaze. She smiled as they walked, looking content.

They started ascending the hill east of her village. She followed as he picked his way through the brush, trying to find a trail. Then he remembered that she was wearing the tightly wrapped dress and hoped it wasn't too difficult for her and that it wouldn't get snagged.

They made their way up the gentle slope and were soon near the crest of the hill. John stopped and looked back from where they had come, and could pick out the village through a gap in the trees.

Perfect, he thought.

He retrieved a set of binoculars from his back pack and trained them on the village. Then he held them out for Meishan and said, "*Look*," in her language.

She hesitated at first, then took what must have seemed an odd looking item and awkwardly placed it up to her face. John helped her aim them down at her village.

She drew in a gasp of air, clearly delighted. She pulled them down from her eyes and looked at her village, then looked through the binoculars again. She said something, then turned the binoculars toward him and giggled like a girl, and pulled them down again, smiling.

"I like," she said.

He smiled back.

The pair walked a little further and found a clearing with some fallen trees and sat down across from one another and tried to have a conversation. It was difficult but fun as they both used the words they knew in each other's language to their fullest extent, stretching their meanings in the process. John could tell that Meishan was speaking slowly and trying to use simple words, since he knew more of her language than she knew English. They both used a lot of exaggerated facial expressions and pantomime to get their message across. It brought them to a common ground.

The sky grew dark as they sat enjoying one another's company. Then the moon rose above some scattered clouds and John decided to pull out the binoculars again. He sat next to her and helped her hold them steady with one hand, his other arm around her back.

Again she gasped and then muttered something softly. Then she said, "Beautiful."

John smiled, it was fun sharing this new experience with her. He got to see things through her eyes. He felt her shoulder in his hand, her smooth dress transmitting the feel of her skin and tone of her muscle. He squeezed it lightly in his hand, enjoying the simple tactile sensation.

After a minute she lowered the glasses and asked him a question, he could make out, "what is the name for?" but not what she was talking about. Then she repeatedly made a circle in the air with her finger.

Oh, he thought and said, "Crater," and held up his hands forming a circle, "Crater."

"Crah-tuw," she said back to him. They exchanged the word back and forth a couple of times until she had it down.

Meishan smiled and looked him in the eyes for a silent moment then said, "Thank you." John understood her to mean that she was thanking him for showing her something she hadn't seen before.

Going back down the hill in the dark wasn't easy, John hadn't thought this part of the date through, other than to bring a flashlight. Use of batteries was supposed to be for emergencies only, but he couldn't very well have the both of them stuck on the hill all night, or falling and breaking a leg.

Meishan marveled at the flashlight, John and the other soldiers had tried to limit how much technology they exposed to the villagers. They didn't want to upset their understanding of the world. But it was difficult to do and couldn't be helped in this case.

Next time, bring a gas lantern, John told himself.

Once down off the hill and out of the trees, the moon provided more than enough light to see by as he walked her home. At her door she turned and said, "I like."

What to do next time? he thought.

Chapter 22: Escalation

Lieutenant Franks sat in the observation post on a chair liberated from camp. It wasn't exactly comfortable, but it would do. He closed his eyes briefly, feeling the sun on his face. It was almost midday and the sun had finally come up over the ridge behind them taking the chill out of the little area that served as their OP.

They weren't expecting any trouble up here on the plateau, so there wasn't a defensive structure of any kind, just a short wall made of fallen logs that more or less defined where the OP was. There was also a small tent where he and his six men took turns sleeping.

For observation they had two sets of binoculars on hand. The first were powerful 25 x 100mm binoculars attached to a heavy tripod. The second was a smaller set of 10 x 50mm Leupold range finding binoculars that were easy to heft around.

Franks typically rotated through the same jobs as his men, to keep focused, but right now was dozing lightly, having been on morning watch at sunup. This was day five, *or was it six?* Of keeping watch over the valley. So far there had been nothing to see except occasional deer passing by.

It had been nearly a week since the confrontation down in the village. If no one came to investigate within another week, it probably wasn't going to happen Lt. Franks reasoned. He closed his eyes again and was reminded of days camping with his brothers. He was temporarily saddened recalling that he would never see them again, but then shrugged it off and just enjoyed the fond memories.

* * *

Private Murphy stood guard at the front of the village near the clinic and the livestock pens. He was tired. Sleeping was difficult in the little shacks of Shanty Town. His bunk mate, Specialist Jones, didn't seem to have a problem sleeping anywhere. *That is the mark of a professional soldier*, he had decided.

This was his second rotation to the village with the guard detail, now a week old. He didn't understand why they didn't just assign a permanent group of guys to handle the duty and cut out someone having to march back and forth from camp every day, but no one had asked for his opinion. His lieutenant had said that it was to give more people the opportunity to see the village, and familiarize themselves with the layout and their neighbors.

Okay, fine, he had thought.

It was a quiet little place. The villagers were a bit standoffish, but wearing his full combat gear he could understand why. Some of them would smile and say a word of greeting, and Matt would reply in kind. All in all he liked the stillness of the village.

Truthfully the duty was getting boring. He understood the need for it, having been briefed about the engagement that had occurred the week before, pretty much right where he now stood. But even if someone showed up, what could they do to match the firepower of the squad? Arrows and sling stones didn't sound particularly scary to him. During basic training they had taught him to be scared of machinegun fire, mortars, and such but they hadn't said anything about arrows.

But someone else thought otherwise as he looked at the fox holes dug into the ground about ten feet away. There was one for each of the guards near their posts, two in this case, complete with covers as falling into one of these in the dark would be a rude surprise indeed.

"Hey Murph."

Matt turned to see Jones walking up, coming back from a trip to the latrine.

"I don't know about you, but this detail ain't so much fun as it sounded," Jones said. "It's small and you can't really talk to the people. Too quiet for me."

Matt smiled and said, "It's not so bad. I'll be glad when our relief gets here though. The bed back at camp isn't great but it's ten times better than sleeping in that shack."

"You just ain't done enough time in field my man. You do enough a this, and you'll be able to sleep in the back of a Bradley goin cross country," Jones said.

I really don't want to acquire that skill, Matt thought.

* * *

Lt. Franks was dozing lightly in his chair, vaguely aware of his surroundings but also having a dream about driving to work as a teenager in his '02 Z28. But in the dream when he got to the pizza place it had turned into a sushi bar. His dream was interrupted by a voice.

"Lieutenant."

Franks opened his eyes and tried to clear the fog from his mind. He got his bearings and looked over to the man talking to him.

"Sir, I see something out on the road, 1,500 meters from the village," Specialist Wilson said somewhat excitedly. "A column of foot soldiers, they are still coming into view but I estimate a company."

Chris Franks' mind was laser focused now, he moved quickly down to Wilson's position and took the binoculars. He could see a large group of men walking in loose ranks carrying something, maybe spears but he couldn't quite tell. They wore black outfits. Then he saw two men on horseback, their manner and actions indicated that they were in charge.

Specialist Needham was sitting ready with a field radio. Franks took it from him and called into it, "Hornet's nest, this is Sky Mountain," the radio call signs for the machinegun position and his OP.

"Hornet's nest, go ahead Sky Mountain," came the reply.

"We've got foot infantry coming down the road, about 1,500 meters from your position. At least company strength, hang on," the lieutenant paused to look at Specialist Wilson.

"Sir, just got the tail of the group, a company of foot bound with hand weapons, and another platoon or so of archers… and looks like… four men on horseback."

The lieutenant returned to the radio, "Add to that a platoon of archers and a few men on horse, probably officers."

"Roger that," came the intense reply, "We are set to engage at 100."

Lt. Franks knew the rules of engagement that had been outlined. They were free to engage any overtly hostile force once it closed to within 100 meters of the village.

Not long now…

* * *

Private Murphy was leaning against the fence at the entrance to the village. The wind had shifted and he was keenly aware of the animal pens nearby. Jones was nearby downing some water.

Then the private heard an air horn sound out, this was the alert signal indicating that there was an attack imminent. His heart jumped. He unslung his rifle and looked out down the road, but saw nothing.

"Holes," Jones said.

They both flipped the wooden covers off of their foxholes and jumped in. This gave them cover up to their chests as they leaned forward, assault rifles trained down the road.

"Remember, wait for the machinegun to open fire before engaging, unless we are under direct attack," Jones instructed, Matt just nodded.

* * *

John Pontus looked at Meishan sitting on the river bank near him, the sun on her face. She was looking out across the river.

She said to him, "I like our walk," in Okor and pointed across the river. John looked at her and realized that she meant their little hike the previous night, when they had walked up onto that mountain.

"I like walk," he replied in agreement.

Then a horn blared. He snapped upright and instinctively turned toward the sound. She was startled by the noise and he took her by the hand, "Come on," he said.

They ran together. He led her away from the village, up the hill toward Shanty Town. He didn't know why this was where he took her, only that he didn't want her to be in the village. He wanted her as far away from harm as possible.

It took only a couple of minutes to get there, and he quickly led her inside a shelter, telling her and motioning for her to stay put. She nodded affirmatively.

Then he sprinted back to the village. It was his duty to be in position before his men had to engage the enemy, but he'd had to get her to safety first. If the attackers were mounted, then he might be late…

As he got closer, he could see that the road was clear, *good*, he thought. He slowed down as he got within shouting distance of the machinegun emplacement and called out to them. A rifleman outside acknowledged him and called back into the pillbox. A moment later Sergeant Paulson appeared.

"A company of foot soldiers, mix of spearmen and archers, halted at 500," the sergeant shouted.

Lt. Pontus shouted back, "Affirmative Sergeant, prepare to engage." Then he turned and ran the rest of the way to the clinic.

They stopped 500 meters away, out of sight of the village… readying their attack, he thought.

Pontus reached the clinic and rounded the building. He saw Specialist Jones and Private Murphy in their foxholes, ready for action. They turned to look at him but kept their rifles trained down the road.

"Lieutenant," Jones said.

"Sorry I took so long. You guys look set. Jones are you on the radio?" Lt. Pontus asked.

Jones lifted it for the lieutenant to see, "What do you know sir?"

"Not much, give me a sitrep," Pontus commanded.

Jones explained the sequence of events, the size and make-up of the force, and that they had halted about a minute prior.

Pontus took it in as he retrieved his rifle, helmet and other equipment from the left side of the village entrance. Then he inspected a set of controls that was there.

"You going to use those L-T?" Jones asked.

The lieutenant shook his head, "No, I don't think we need them for this. It's a relatively small and slow force. I was more concerned about stopping a cavalry charge," and he set the box down.

He walked over to Jones and knelt down taking the radio, "Sky Mountain this is Position One."

"Go ahead Position One," came the reply.

"Give me an updated picture," John commanded.

A voice replied, "We have approximately 120 foot soldiers. 100 armed with some kind of short narrow pointed spear or axe, not sure what they are exactly. The other 20 are archers. The archers just started moving, heading off the road, looks like they are going to try and flank the village on the right."

"Okay, keep an eye on those, the other ones aren't too concerning," the lieutenant said.

"Roger that. We also have four on horseback they are having a little meeting right now at the tail of the formation," the voice added.

Behind him the lieutenant heard others approaching. He saw the young villager with his short sword, three older men with bows and another three with slings. Cong and Kuson were with them and so was one of the interpreters in training.

Pontus appreciated that this was their village and their willingness to fight, but he didn't want to have to worry about their safety, and he really didn't need them and their weapons on this occasion.

"You should get inside and stay safe, let us handle this," he said, hoping the interpreter could get that idea across.

The interpreter said something and Kuson shook his head, walking forward, saying something John couldn't make out. The interpreter said in English, "He is leader, he be here."

Pontus looked at the elder man and nodded in respect, "Of course."

"Lieutenant Pontus," came a voice on the radio.

"Go ahead," he replied.

"You've got two men on horseback approaching the village now at a light gallop, no weapons evident. Looks like they might want to talk," the voice from the observation team relayed. "And the rest of the formation has started walking again at an easy pace."

"Okay, roger that," he said into the radio, then turning to Jones and Murphy said, "button up." The two enlisted men complied, getting down low and pulling the covers over their foxholes.

Lastly he turned toward Kuson, raised two fingers and said, "Two men coming on horseback."

The interpreter relayed the message and Kuson nodded and walked forward toward the fence. He motioned to the armed villagers, said something to them, and they backed away up against the clinic out of sight. Pontus joined them.

John heard the horses clearly now, he peeked and saw the two riders approaching. They were dressed like the previous riders they had met, wearing dark leather.

They came to a stop and both dismounted. Kuson approached them and a conversation started.

Kuson greeted them calmly, and one of the men responded in kind. The man asked Kuson something. Kuson replied, again calmly and John was pretty sure he was answering in the negative.

The warrior asked another question, this time John could pick out the word for horse. Kuson again responded negatively. The rider said something curtly. Then he and the other man walked back to their horses, mounted them and rode off at a gallop.

Lt. Pontus walked back out to where Kuson stood wondering what had been said. The interpreter spoke, "He question we have horses. Kuson say 'no'. He say lie."

The lieutenant considered this, *clever guy, he must have seen some sign that the others had been here last week.* John hadn't really expected that they would be able to just feign ignorance and make them go away, but it was worth a try.

Into the radio, John said, "Okay men, let's be ready."

Jones and Murphy popped out of their foxholes, sliding the covers aside.

A voice on the radio from the OP announced that the foot troops were within 300 meters now, and the archers were paralleling them at the same pace and would soon gain cover from a small rise covered with brush.

Lt. Pontus just waited. He stood around the corner of the clinic for cover, he didn't have a fox hole, and soon saw the head of the foot column, 200 meters away right to where the grass had been cut. He wondered if they would charge, or just walk in not really expecting anyone to challenge them.

"The archers have halted advance about 150 meters from your position," came the voice on the radio.

John couldn't see them from where he stood, but replied, "Roger that."

He could see the approaching warriors clearly now. Their armor was similar to that of the riders, simple leather, but they also wore leather helmets. They held pole weapons in their right hands leaned up against the shoulder just like a soldier with a rifle. The weapons were approximately one meter in length and topped by a metal head piece that had the appearance of a small pick axe.

They were almost at the 100 meter engagement line, and John found himself wavering. *This will be a slaughter.* But he realized the only alternative was to let them raze the village, which they appeared intent on doing. You don't march a group of armed warriors out into the boonies for tea.

The front rank was now 100 meters away. "Hornet's Nest, open fire," he said into the radio.

Two seconds after he gave the order the air was filled with a grating sound from the M240 machine gun located in the bunker across the river. John couldn't see it from where he stood but saw its effects almost immediately. Men fell to the ground amid shouts and cries, dust was stirred up and fear and confusion spread rapidly in their ranks.

Faster though was the stream of .30 caliber bullets cutting them down, which occasionally paused for a few seconds before starting anew. Lt. Pontus saw the last rows disperse, some fleeing and others diving to the ground. 50 meters of ground was covered with men and even from this distance John could see the blood and hear their screaming, it was sickening.

* * *

After the two horsemen had left, Murphy and Jones had popped their heads back out of their foxholes, glad to get fresh air again.

But when the machine gun opened fire, Private Murphy found himself ducking back down in his foxhole instinctively. Then cautiously he raised his head and saw the damage being done to the men down the road. He had never seen anything like it and had to look away.

Then he saw something over in the valley to his right. Several small objects flying quickly through the air. *Arrows?*

"Jones, Murphy move up and put some fire on those archers," he heard the order from Lt. Pontus. A moment later, the machine gun fire stopped.

Jones popped up and motioned for Murphy to come with him. They kept low and ran up to where the livestock pens ended. From there, they could see a dozen or more archers behind a small hill that was protecting them from the machinegun fire.

Jones laid his M4 carbine across the top of the wooden fence and took aim, Murphy did likewise. He heard the report from Jones' rifle firing one shot at a time. The private saw one archer fall and he picked one out for himself, hardly believing this was really happening. He aimed and fired at a range of a little over 100 meters, and hit his target, a *person*, with ease.

The archers ducked down and Private Murphy had trouble making them out from the brush, so he held his fire. Then in unison the archers rose up and let loose a volley of arrows, and they were pointing right at he and Jones!

"Duck!" he found himself yelling.

Within another second the arrows began to fall almost in unison, it was like a tiny hailstorm. He heard them impacting the ground, the fence, and he heard Jones cry out. Looking to his right, he saw that Jones had a bamboo shaft sticking up out of his shoulder. A small amount of blood was seeping out where Jones was clutching the base of the arrow and fighting the pain.

Then Murphy heard a voice yell, "Stay down!" And then it dawned on him that the archers weren't finished with them yet.

Another staccato rapping all around him and then a hard *thunk* right on top of his Kevlar helmet. It made his ears ring, but he didn't feel any pain.

He knew that he only had a few seconds before another volley might fall. He started moving his body while his mind caught up. Under the barrel of his M4 rifle was a 40mm M203 grenade launcher. It had a high explosive shell already loaded.

Standing he trained the weapon on the group of archers who he could see were just drawing another set of arrows. He adjusted his aim slightly and pulled the trigger, heard and felt the thud as the grenade left its tube, then ducked back down right next to Jones, holding his rifle over the top of his wounded friend.

Even at 100 meters away, the sound of the exploding grenade was impressively loud. Private Murphy braced himself for another slew of arrows, but none came. Then he saw Lt. Pontus running up, firing full-automatic bursts from his M4 in the direction of the archers.

"Move it!" the lieutenant yelled as he fired.

Private Murphy stood and pulled Jones up with him. Together they ran back to find cover in the village.

Murphy led Jones toward the clinic and leaned him up against the wall there. Jones was doing okay, but clearly in a lot of pain. Next thing he knew, the lieutenant joined them and looked at Jones' wound.

Matt Murphy sat back, heart racing, pulse pounding in his ears. The engagement had only lasted a minute or two from the time he left his foxhole, but it felt like he had just sprinted a mile.

He saw the doctor and a medic come out of the clinic and hurry to Jones' side. Murphy just laid his head back against the wall and tried to breathe slowly. The lieutenant knelt down beside him.

"You did good Private, quick thinking on your part," the lieutenant said, "you sit tight."

Murphy didn't know what to think or how to feel about that. He hadn't *thought* at all, he had just reacted.

He heard occasional rifle fire in the distance, and then relative quiet. As his ears stopped ringing he started hearing pitiful cries from the wounded men just a short distance down the road. He found himself wishing that the machinegun fire would resume just to drown out the noise.

* * *

Lt. Pontus walked away from his men at the clinic and ducked down to where he could see down the road. He called to the OP on his radio, "Sky Mountain, tell me what you see."

A voice came back, "About twenty of the foot soldiers have made it down around the bend in the road. Some wounded. As I'm sure you can see, the remaining foot soldiers are torn up and lying on the ground."

Lieutenant Pontus nodded and spoke, "Yes, continue."

The voice resumed, "The archers scattered after the explosion, now they've formed up again and are retreating through the brush. Do you want us to engage? Specialist Wilson has a battle rifle."

"Negative. The attack is repelled and I don't have orders to pursue," he paused. "What about the men on horseback?"

"They hung around for less than a minute once the M-G opened fire, then fled. No sign of them now," came the reply.

Inspiring leadership, John thought.

"Alright, keep your eyes open and let me know if anything changes," the lieutenant said.

His gaze shifted toward the mass of bleeding men, some dead, most wounded. He realized then that he had no plan for what to do with them. No way to help that many people with just one doctor and a couple of medics, and nowhere to put them.

Calling back into the radio he said, "Come in Sky Mountain."

After a brief pause, "Sky Mountain here."

"Contact Colonel Erickson and brief him on the engagement. Tell him we need medics, supplies and soldiers for prisoner detail. We have roughly 40 wounded," Pontus ordered.

"Yes sir," was the reply.

The rest of the village guard squad had gathered at his position and he turned to face them. "Specialist Jones was hit by arrow fire, but should be fine. The remnants of the enemy formation are withdrawing. We are going to assist the wounded until help arrives from Camp Nowhere."

Dr. Stone approached the group, "I've got field dressings and other bandages here in the clinic. I'm afraid that given our limited resources we'll need to do a reverse triage and take care of the most lightly injured first," he said gravely. "But I will take a look at some of the more serious injuries and see if there are any I think I can save."

John said, "You heard him, let's move." Then picking out two of his soldiers he said, "You two keep your rifles with you and keep a lookout for trouble makers. We'll separate out the walking wounded and park them over there," pointing to a section of the livestock corral.

The other three soldiers, including Private Murphy, leaned their rifles up on the fence and went to gather the medical supplies.

* * *

Lang stood near the clinic, looking out at the devastation that had been wrought upon the warlord's men. He was mesmerized by the power these green men wielded. There was much commotion right now as they ran out toward the wounded soldiers. *To execute them no doubt*, he thought.

He quietly removed his sword and sheath from his back and dropped them onto the ground, eyes locked onto his goal as he took a step.

He had not planned it, but here was an opportunity that wouldn't come again. As he got closer, guilt tried to dissuade him. He was grateful for what the green men had done for him and the village, but he wanted more. He wanted to be like them, even at risk of death.

Walking slowly, he looked around and didn't see anyone take notice of him. He removed his loose shirt, leaving him bare chested.

Just a few more steps.

As he reached the three long black objects he leaned down and picked up the one on the right, finding its weight similar to an axe. Wrapping his shirt around it he continued walking, expecting someone to shout or to be struck down by some mystical force but nothing happened.

He suppressed a smile as he moved swiftly into the village towards his home, clutching his prize so tightly that it hurt his chest. He had one thought running through his mind.

I have a thunder bow!

Chapter 23: Carnage

Colonel Erickson stood looking down the road, where many bodies lay and the ground was covered with blood. He had a sick feeling in his stomach, not from the gore, which he could detach from, but at the loss of life, and the nature of the engagement. It had been a defensive action, but these men didn't have any chance whatsoever in the face of weaponry they could have scarcely imagined. It was a massacre.

He noticed Major Baker walk up beside him but he didn't speak. After a moment of shared silence, the colonel said, "Yes major?"

"Sir, we've got more body bags coming up shortly. I'm still waiting for your direction regarding the bodies, whether they are to be stripped of uniform or not," the major said somberly.

Erickson replied, "I think we should remove the evidence of these soldiers for the village's protection, even if ends up being in vain. But their leader wants the leather. Best I can understand, it would be a useful resource for them." He sighed and then stated decisively. "So, that is what we will do. I assume that the deceased have something on under the armor. That will have to suffice for their burial."

Major Dan Baker nodded and turned to walk away, then the colonel added, "Make sure the locals who are assisting are respectful in their handling of the victims, uh dead," he corrected himself.

The major gave a slight smile of understanding and replied in the affirmative that he would see that it was done.

Colonel Erickson walked back into the village proper and saw two boys making piles of weapons that had been removed from the warriors. There was no question that the villagers could find uses for the bronze implements. Erickson had decided to take several back to Camp Nowhere to show the rest of the unit. It's good to know the weapons of your potential enemy. But he also had an eye toward the future knowing that there would be no way to replace their ammunition once it was gone. Though, the ammo they did have would likely last a lifetime.

Unless Genghis Khan comes knocking, he thought.

Two other boys were carrying one of the dead soldiers in a fabric sling of sorts. The villagers were carrying the bodies and lining them up out near Shanty Town. From there, his soldiers were placing them into body bags and carrying them back to where a truck was parked, not too far around the hill.

One of the projects that the colonel had commissioned was creating a road to go all the way to the village. It had been cleared of trees and bushes, mostly by hand, but no other improvements had been made thus far as it would mainly see foot traffic, diesel fuel would run out long before ammo. But he also had known it was likely he'd want to bring vehicles close to the village at some point, as was the case today.

Later that day Colonel Erickson went to the clinic to speak with Dr. Stone. There were ten or so wounded warriors sitting outside on the ground, their armor removed, being guarded by four of his soldiers. From the looks of them, these were the light casualties and most seemed to be enduring their pain well. They didn't seem likely to cause trouble the way they kept looking at the soldiers, as if they were being guarded by Cerberus himself.

For the first time Erickson noticed that not all of the warriors had the black snake emblem impressed onto their right forearm. Of the ten men here seven had the mark. He made a mental note of that then walked into the clinic.

Inside the small clinic he saw six of the enemy lying on mats with bandages affixed to various parts of their bodies. Major Stone was standing next to one of his soldiers, presumably Specialist Jones the lone casualty from the unit. He had his arm in a sling and was sitting on a chair.

The Colonel addressed his young soldier, "How are you doing Specialist?"

"It's pretty sore sir, but I'll manage."

"Colonel, you'd like to know the condition of our guests I assume," the doctor said walking over. "The six in here all have serious injuries. All of them but one are stable," he lowered his voice slightly. "The other one won't make it much longer."

Erickson nodded his understanding. "What about the ones outside?"

"They are all ambulatory," came the response.

"Good, good," the colonel nodded again. "They're going to be taking a walk first thing in the morning."

The doctor's face showed a brief moment of surprise, but replied simply, "That should be fine Colonel."

"Good to hear. Well I won't take any more of your time, you obviously have your hands full," the colonel said. Hearing someone else enter the room, he turned to see Major Baker.

"Colonel, can I have a moment," the major requested.

"Yes Major," Erickson replied as he started to walk to the door.

Together they left the clinic and the colonel walked out toward the river into the afternoon sunlight, and away from anyone else that might hear their discussion. Once they were well away from the clinic, Erickson said, "Go ahead Major."

"Sir, I'd like you to give more consideration into the idea of sending a heavily armed assault force to locate and destroy the enemy camp, or town or whatever it is," Major Baker said.

Earlier that day Colonel Erickson had told his officers his plan to let some of the prisoners go in the hopes that they would lead them to their base camp. He wanted to shadow them with a small reconnaissance force so they could gather as much information about them as possible.

The major had been quick to suggest sending a follow on force with the intention of attacking and destroying whatever was there. Though a reasonable idea, Colonel Erickson had rejected it. He had no doubt that a platoon sized group of men could decimate the enemy with minimal or no losses, and that was one of his problems with it.

It's not that Colonel Erickson didn't have the stomach for the job, his was a unit for making war after all, it's that his conscience was nagging at him. They weren't at war and he didn't want to become a tyrant, wielding unstoppable power the likes of which *this* world at *this* time had never seen. It made him feel godlike, and he didn't want to decide whose time it was to live or die.

"No Major, I'm not considering that course of action at this time. We'll find out more about them, where they are, and their numbers. We'll obtain the information we need to carry out such an attack mission in the future, *if* it becomes necessary."

The major's face showed his disappointment.

"I've got more information on the two deserters," he said plainly. "They definitely aren't in the camp, and not here in the village either," Major Baker began. "Their gear is missing, including weapons. Not sure what else they took, could be just about anything that isn't locked up. Certainly they would have taken some food. I have no idea where they would have headed."

"We're also missing a rifle from here in the village. I don't know if this is related to the deserters, they weren't on village duty but I suppose they could have swung through and lifted it. That was a hectic day," Baker said.

The colonel scratched his chin and mulled this over. There really wasn't much to do about it. He didn't feel like having someone try to chase them down as that might end poorly.

"We need to secure the weapons, including sidearms. Have them checked in and out, ammo too. Just like when we are on base during peace time," the colonel stated. "There isn't any imminent threat back at camp, so only those on guard duty should have weapons. Anyone assigned to activity away from camp can also be issued small arms."

The major took it in nodding, "Yes sir."

Colonel Erickson resumed, "I think we need to accelerate our plans to make a more permanent settlement. Hopefully that will give the men a sense of purpose and reduce boredom. They've got too much time to think right now, we need to fix that."

Major Baker smiled slightly at this, "I agree Colonel."

Erickson started walking again, heading toward the river.

"How many men do you want to send out on the scout mission?" Major Baker asked.

The colonel turned to him and replied, "I'm going to have Lieutenant Pontus lead the mission. We'll send a total of six, plus one of the villagers, one of the interpreters might come in handy. I spoke to Kuson and he seemed enthusiastic about the idea."

"I'm worried that only six men could find themselves overwhelmed if they come into contact with the enemy," the major opined.

Colonel Erickson's voice grew stern, "Then they better damn well not get into contact with the enemy! I'll make that point crystal clear with the lieutenant."

The colonel knew that defending the village with prepared positions was one thing. Going on offense, even if the mission was just collecting information, was much more unpredictable and dangerous. Anything could happen out in the wild.

Chapter 24: Follow the Leader

Lieutenant Pontus held up his hand and brought his small team to a stop. They were already stooped over, and now pushed themselves even lower to the ground. The ten men they were following had come to a halt. In their black uniforms they were easy to spot even 200 meters down the hill Pontus and his men were on.

His group of seven included Sergeant Turner and Private Murphy, both of whom had performed well in combat with the enemy. They were also extremely fit, as were the three other soldiers he had handpicked for the detail.

Gan, a villager around 13 years old, was the seventh man on the team, one of the interpreters. John was surprised that he was the one the village leader had selected for the job, so young for a potentially dangerous mission. But in the past few hours since they had set out at sun up he had shown that he was as fleet as a deer. He wouldn't be slowing the group down.

As an added benefit Gan was a hunter with adept tracking skills. About 30 minutes after leaving the village, the boy had spotted tracks of a single person heading toward the village. The lieutenant had been tempted to have one of his men follow them, but there wasn't time as they needed to keep up with the group of released prisoners. Instead he had called it in to the OP and proceeded with their mission.

The warriors weren't in a particular hurry which was good, as they had the benefit of walking along a valley that was free of obstacles. John's team was not so lucky. He wanted to keep his team at a higher elevation to take advantage of the bright sun that would have the wounded column of men keeping their eyes down. He also wanted the cover offered by the trees and bushes found on the slopes. With all that plus their camouflaged uniforms and painted faces, the risk of being spotted was almost nil as long as they kept their distance. Noise was probably their biggest enemy, as such they proceeded carefully.

Lt. Pontus estimated that they had traveled a distance of eight kilometers. Until now the men they were following had mostly kept moving, only stopping occasionally to relieve themselves. But now, watching through his compact spotting monocular, he could see that two of them were having a heated discussion. One of the men was pointing to the arm of the second. This man held it up showing him... *what?* Then John realized they were talking about the man's wounded arm.

Prior to letting the prisoners leave the village this morning, they had all received three gifts. First, they were fed. Second they were given back their black leather armor. Lastly, all of their bandages were replaced with materials gathered up from within the village. The gauze, bandages and band aids were all removed. These items clearly were not something that existed in this world, and so all evidence of them had been removed.

"What are they doing Lieutenant?" he heard Turner ask with a hushed voice.

Pontus turned to him and cracked a smile, speaking softly, "I think they're trying to get their stories straight." John returned to watching their quarry, "I'd like to hear that story myself."

The lieutenant turned and huddled with his team, "It looks like these guys are sorting themselves out. That tells me that they're probably close to home. Keep an eye out around you, we could quickly find ourselves within the perimeter of a town or camp, stay sharp," he implored. He received nods all around.

After a few more minutes, the wounded men resumed their loose march. Lt. Pontus waited a minute and then got his group moving again as well. After 20 minutes of walking the men they were following headed off the trail, uphill and away from where his group was. This necessitated moving the group down into the valley so they could continue following.

This was the riskiest movement they'd had to make all day and they lost sight of the black clad warriors in the process. But Lt. Pontus wasn't worried about finding them again, they had made no effort at evasion all day. The ten of them hadn't talked a lot, but made quite a lot of noise just moving through the brush.

As Lieutenant Pontus crested a ridge, he froze. Ahead of him was a large plateau, at least 1,500 meters across, upon which there were several small structures, and a roughly built wooden corral.

The ten men they had been following were about 200 meters ahead, just entering the camp. Beyond them were several other men dressed as they were. He saw a couple of horses tied up as well.

John turned and motioned for his team to come up and have a look, but had them stay low. He again took out his mono scope to get a better look. The leader of the ten was talking very excitedly with one of the men in the camp, the only one not wearing armor at present, presumably an officer. This exchange went on for several minutes.

The armor-less man brought the discussion to a close and appeared to issue an order to the others. The ten moved off toward one of the small buildings with the officer. The remaining soldiers walked toward the corral area. It was then that John first noticed movement from within the fenced in area and was surprised to see first one, then several men stand up. They wore plain clothes, similar those worn by the villagers, and looked to be bound at the hands and tied to the fence.

John concluded that this was a camp where they brought the conscripts to be held prior to being taken elsewhere. The camp was large enough to hold many more people so he surmised that this was the last of the current class of recruits.

Over the next hour, the men in the camp gathered up belongings, equipment and supplies. The conscripts were untied from the fence and given something small to eat.

Checking his watch it was almost noon, and the lieutenant wondered how long it would take to get to the next stop. If it was him moving prisoners, he wouldn't want to make camp again unless it was necessary. He motioned for Corporal Jenkins to come with him as he scrambled down the slope about 20 meters.

PFC Jenkins was carrying their only heavy item, a backpack which housed a powerful wireless two-way radio. Lt. Pontus switched it on and lifted the handset.

"This is Wayward Sons calling Sky Mountain," the lieutenant spoke and then waited.

"This is Sky Mountain," came the voice of his friend Lt. Franks.

He described the situation at the camp and that they would likely be on the move again shortly.

"We'll check back in around 1800." With that he switched the radio off walked back up the hill.

Sergeant Turner said, "You haven't missed much Lieutenant."

Lieutenant Pontus nodded and said, "If they all leave, we'll take a few minutes to check out the camp before following."

He resumed observing the activity in the camp just in time to see the officer appear out of one of the small covered structures, now wearing his armor. With him were two other people whose hands were bound. From their clothes they appeared to be villagers, and then John realized they were... *women*.

Pontus turned to the others and whispered, "Two *female* conscripts."

He decided then and there that he didn't like these guys very much. As John thought this over more, he decided that his surprise merely showed how naïve he was. This wasn't a liberated society like 21st Century America, it was an ancient culture in a faraway land.

No one back in the village had mentioned anything about the soldiers taking women out of the village, only men. Either it hadn't happened to them, or they just didn't want to talk about it. John then pictured Meishan being taken, and felt an anger rise.

The motley group before them began to move. John took a final count, 14 armed soldiers walking plus 2 on horseback , 7 male and 2 female prisoners tied at the hands and then tied to each other by a long rope, 25 in total.

The group started heading east and soon were descending the other side of the plateau. Lt. Pontus waited until he could no longer see the men on horseback, who were at the rear of the loose column. They had more than a thousand meters head start, but John wasn't worried about losing or catching them, they would be easy to track.

"Alright, let's split up and look through these buildings. Let's head out in five minutes," the lieutenant ordered.

The seven stood upright and fanned out across the camp. The young interpreter stayed close to John. John reminded himself, not for the first time that day, that the boy didn't understand much of what he said but seemed to get the general idea pretty well.

The lieutenant wanted to look at the building the officer came out of. He wasn't sure what he was hoping to find, but it seemed like the right thing to do.

As he got to within five meters of the door, a man appeared in the doorway. He was of average height for the local Koreans but seemed much broader through the middle. He wore the same black armor as the soldiers that had just left. His eyes grew wide as he saw John and a piece of food fell out of his gaped mouth.

John's heart raced in an instant, he knew he had screwed this up royally, but he pushed that thought aside focusing on the man. In the stalemate of surprise, it was his adversary that acted first.

"Yahhhh…" the man yelled in alarm.

Pontus simultaneously dropped his rifle, began sprinting and drew his knife. The man reached for the sword hanging from his hip just as John tackled him bringing up the knife and plunging it cleanly into his throat.

133

The rest of John's squad turned when they heard the man yell. They too were transfixed at the sight, and then Sergeant Turner shouted.

"Get down!"

In the entryway to the small building, John lay on top of the man, left hand clamped across his mouth while his right held the blade that was deep inside his neck. After a few more moments, the smaller man's struggling stopped.

John slowly released his grip on him and got up but left the knife behind.

The sergeant came to the building and looked his lieutenant over.

"You alright sir?"

Not waiting for a response the sergeant approached and checked the man's pulse.

Pontus tried to regain his breath and shake off the sudden and violent nature of what had just happened.

"Yeah, I'm alright Sergeant."

The lieutenant surveyed the rest of the room confirming no one else was there. Then his brain started catching up.

"The other buildings?" was the vague question.

"The men are watching them, I've got them down in the weeds until we're sure that no one in that group heard this guy yell or comes back looking for him," the sergeant replied.

Lieutenant Pontus nodded his approval. Just outside he saw the young villager lying in the grass, his eyes locked on John.

After two minutes that seemed like 20, no one appeared out of the remaining buildings, and none of the traveling party came back. Pontus was thankful on both counts. He couldn't shake the knowledge that he'd screwed this up, but it looked like it wasn't going to blow their mission.

The soldiers slowly approached and cleared each of the remaining buildings to ensure no other surprises awaited them. Then they quickly looked them over and found nothing of interest. Just some supplies and implements of ancient life, along with a few unremarkable looking weapons.

The dead man messed things up a bit. They needed to dispose of him quickly. The lieutenant didn't want the opposition to know there was someone running around killing their warriors. Two of his men carried the body off away from the trails they knew of, and dumped it down in some thick brush.

That just left the big pool of blood outside the small building. One of the men used a small folding shovel to scoop up the blood dirt mixture and put it onto a flat piece of wood scavenged from one of the buildings. It too went down the side of the hill.

What John wanted to be a five minute ransacking turned into a 20 minute tangent. They'd have to run to catch up, while still being careful not to give themselves away.

Chapter 25: Fort Wilderness

It hadn't been difficult for Lieutenant Pontus and his men to catch up with the traveling party they were pursuing. The collection of soldiers and prisoners moved along at a steady pace, but John and his fleet-footed group made up the ground within an hour.

After that, it was just a matter of staying in loose contact and avoiding detection. This too had been easy, the large group of men, and women, made a lot of noise moving through the wooded area. They were following an established trail, but it was still bordered with fresh growth of bushes and trees which they inevitably strayed into.

The pursuit went on for a few hours with only an occasional stop for water in or water out. The terrain was a lot of ups and downs as they skirted along valleys and occasionally crested ridges with several hundred foot elevation changes.

Then Lt. Pontus sensed a change in the group they were following. Their pace quickened slightly and their body language indicated to him that they were close to their destination.

The trees thinned out and John had his group slow and drop down into a crawl. They approached the edge of a tree line, after which was a large clearing. They all inched up so they could see what lay beyond.

About one hundred meters into the clearing there was a large fort wall about three meters high made of vertical logs. John estimated it to be one hundred meters long and almost that many wide. Inside the fort at the intersection of these two walls was a covered guard tower, with two men visible inside.

Looking at his map, the lieutenant saw that they were getting out of the mountainous region and were within 20 kilometers of the eastern coast of the Korean Peninsula.

Outside of the fort was the group they had been following for the past couple of hours. They were being met by several other black clad warriors. Pontus, using his spotting scope, was focused on them to see what would happen next. The group of male prisoners, escorted by the bulk of the traveling party, was led around the outside of the fort where he eventually lost sight of them.

The two female prisoners were taken by their two remaining travel companions up to a gate on the shorter side of the fort. The gate was roughly in the middle of the wall about ten meters wide and currently open, with two guards standing post.

The lieutenant was frustrated now, because from his vantage point he couldn't see through the gate or over the fence. He had no idea what the inside of the fort looked like. Besides the guard tower, he could just make out the top of one large building.

John was considering his next move when he heard the sound of bushes rustling behind him too far away to be anyone in his group. He lowered his scope slowly, and glanced out the corner of his eye. Ten meters away stood a man in black armor and he was facing John and his men.

John's heart raced he thought about how to take him out quickly and quietly. But as he turned his head and got a better look at their visitor, relief washed over him.

The man was very intent on the task of emptying his bladder onto a bush, and gave no impression that he had a care about anything else in the world at that moment. A few seconds later, he re-girded his loins and moved off in the opposite direction.

The lieutenant gave a slight smile as he met the gaze of Sergeant Turner.

But after the relief came concern, they had been caught unaware because they were all so focused on the fort. It was their second mistake of the day, *his* second mistake of the day. The next one could cost one of his men their life.

They were in a bad position. Not only could they not see what was going on in the fort, the opposition evidently patrolled the woods, or liked to go for nature hikes in their spare time. Either way it was no good.

Pontus and his group of seven spent the next 30 minutes back tracking slowly and quietly. Once it felt like they were a safe distance away, John talked to his men.

"I want to get a look inside that place, ideas?" the lieutenant asked.

The men all looked at each other, except for Corporal Jenkins who was looking up.

"I can climb one of these trees and see what I can see sir," Jenkins said dispassionately.

The lieutenant just handed the corporal his monocular and said, "Take this, and the camera." Pontus turned to Sergeant Turner who produced a Nikon digital SLR camera with a long lens.

The sergeant turned the camera on and adjusted some settings, looking through the eyepiece when he was done. He handed it over to Jenkins and said, "Here, just leave it on, it'll wake itself up when you push the button. Don't mess with any of the settings or you might end up having the flash go off." Turner pointed to the button that controlled the shutter. And showed him the ring on the lens that controlled zoom.

Jenkins looked at the sergeant with concern for a moment, then put the camera into the case that the sergeant handed over. Lt. Pontus helped Jenkins take his radio pack off, and he pointed to one of the other men in the group to take it.

The lieutenant watched Rod Jenkins crawl closer to the fort and select a large tree that had a full set of leaves. He discarded his boots, and scrambled up into the tree.

The rest of the group just lay still as the sky started to grow dark above them.

After about ten minutes, Lieutenant Pontus saw some branches moving, and then down to the ground dropped Jenkins.

After the corporal retrieved his boots and crawled back over, they huddled up as a group.

"Any trouble up there?" the lieutenant asked.

Jenkins shook his head, "No sir. I got a few good pictures I think, but the angle still wasn't great and all those leaves made it difficult plus it's getting dark."

He handed the camera to the sergeant who said, "We don't want to risk looking at these here, the screen is pretty bright, someone might see it."

Lt. Pontus nodded his agreement and Jenkins pulled out a piece of paper and pencil then started sketching out a diagram of the compound. Pontus produced a flashlight with a red filter to minimize the risk of anyone spotting them.

"Before I get to the fort itself, up there I was able to see down into the valley on the right. Close by is a large encampment that appears military in nature but I couldn't see it clearly. On the far side of the valley there is what looks like a small town, say three or four times as big as our village."

"Now the fort is roughly a rectangle, about 100 by 70 meters," the corporal said. "Besides the outer fence, there is a shorter inner fence that splits the compound up about 80 percent 20 percent. I'll come back to that."

"Along this long side wall, there are four roughly identical single story buildings, looks like barracks. I saw a number of men walking in and out of them. Over on the right there are a few other buildings of various sizes."

"The largest building is along the far wall," Jenkins said pointing to his map. "It might be as many as 50 meters long, and as you could see before it's a two story structure. It butts up against the outer wall facing the valley."

Jenkins continued, "This building has a higher quality look to it compared to the others, so figure it's the boss' house. There were some guards stationed outside it at different points."

"Getting back to that fence in the courtyard, it's not as tall as this outer fence, it's about head high, figure two meters. It has two gates, one large, one small. There is one building that I could see inside the smaller courtyard. Roughly the size of one of the barracks buildings, but it has a different look. It has some ornate designs or carvings on the face and top. One of them looked like a large animal, like a cow or pig, it was really hard for me to make out the details. Kind of big, round and squat," Jenkins motioned as he spoke.

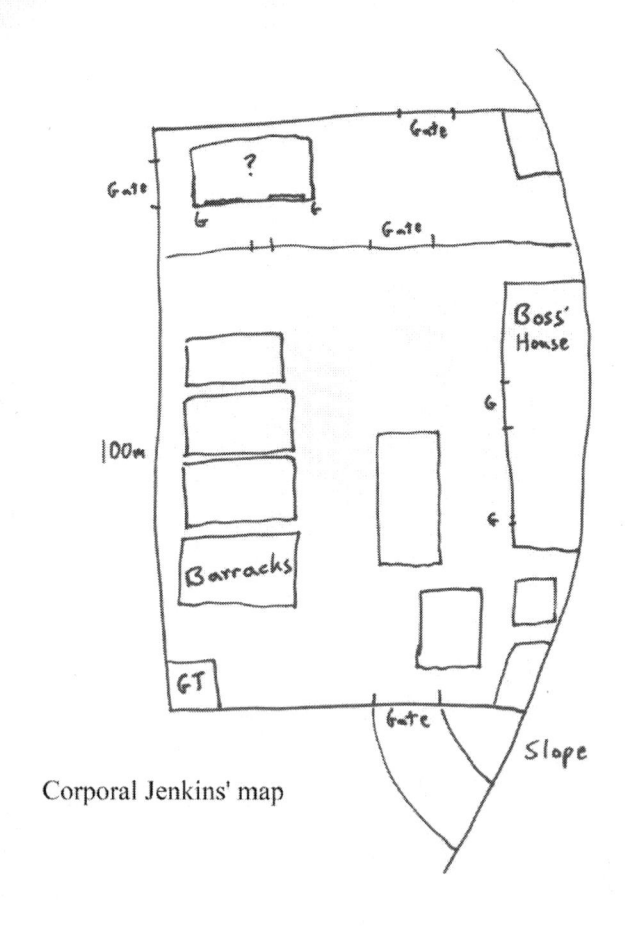

Corporal Jenkins' map

John nodded, "Good report Jenkins. Anything else that might be useful?"

Corporal Jenkins grimaced and replied, "There is something odd about the construction of the buildings, but I can't put my finger on it."

"Okay team, it'll be dark soon then we can get on with it. Until then, get some rest and fuel up."

John took his own advice and munched on some crackers and chicken chunks from an MRE. It had been a busy day and before he knew it, darkness had come.

"Alright men," the lieutenant whispered, "Jenkins hasn't been able to reach anyone on the radio, probably too many mountains in the way, so we'll need to head back soon and check in. But first, I want to scout the other side of that fort, and take a peek at the camp down in the valley."

He looked at the group, "Murphy, you and me."

The two dropped off most of their gear, just taking the sound suppressed sub-machinegun from Sergeant Turner and their night vision goggles.

John led the way through the brush, using his night vision goggles. As he picked his way from tree to bush he held tightly onto the H&K MP5 sub-machinegun that had a silencer built into the front of it. This made the weapon much quieter when fired compared to a regular gun. The difference between a really big firecracker and dropping a book on the ground.

Private Murphy and Lt. Pontus steadily made their way toward the fort, they would go around its right side, where the ground started sloping away into the valley.

As they emerged from under cover of the trees, the two men took off their night vision goggles. The moon helped human eyes just as it helped night vision, and there was the real danger that if someone was looking in their direction, they would be spotted. Having the goggles off gave them a better sense of the risk of detection, and restored their peripheral vision.

They saw no one as they got within 50 meters of the fort. Pontus saw the ground changed ahead it was mostly devoid of vegetation, a dirt road. It led up to the gate in the fort wall, the same gate the captive women had been taken through earlier in the day. Down to their right, the road led into the valley.

They kept moving and were soon in a more secluded position, just a few meters from the fort wall facing the valley. They quietly moved down almost the full length of the exterior wall until they had the vantage point that Pontus wanted. There in the valley below he saw what looked to be a military camp, he couldn't think of how else to describe it. It was much larger than the fort but was surrounded by a similar rectangular palisade style fence.

Donning his night vision Pontus could see the camp was packed with lots of small structures. There were two types that he could make out. The first type were solid looking and regular, similar to the buildings inside the fort behind him. The other type were nothing more than crude three walled huts with a light covering for a roof, like small shacks.

Based on the size of the camp, John was trying to estimate the number of warriors that were based there. By capacity alone, the camp could probably hold around 2,000 men but it seemed too quiet to be housing that many at present.

On the far side of the camp were stables for horses. John could make the animals out with more clarity because the stables didn't have any overhead cover. He estimated around 50 horses with stall room for many more.

Then something caught his ears. He turned to look back at the tall wall behind him, and thought he heard a scream.

He tapped Murphy on the shoulder and indicated that he was going to move up closer to the fence. Removing his night vision he crept up to the wall.

Another scream, that of a woman or a child. It made Pontus' skin twinge. The fence construction was such that he couldn't see through it. The gaps had been well filled in with an earthen mortar. He kept looking and noticed a small beam of light escaping from between two of the posts a few feet away.

John scooted along and squinted through the sliver of a gap. He could just see the end of the two story building and a closed door. There was a guard standing just outside the door and a small fire burned on a pedestal a few feet in front of him.

The lieutenant pulled out his knife and worked it into the small gap to improve his peep hole. Then he leaned over and peered through just in time to see the door fling open.

The light was dim, but he saw a small person stumble out, an instant later he realized it was a woman. In the light of the fire her naked body glowed softly on one side, starkly contrasted with dark shadows on the other. She was crying hysterically.

The guard laughed as she took a few stumbling steps away from the open door toward the fence.

Then a man came out of the door. He was wearing only a loincloth, and even in the faint light John could see his scowl. He ran after the young woman and grabbed her by her short, disheveled hair. She let out a cry of pain as he turned her around, leading her back toward the door, pulling her arm and pushing on the back of her head.

John's thumb twitched lightly on the safety of his gun as he imagined squeezing off one round into the back of the man's skull.

Just as the two got within a few feet of the door, another man came out. At first John thought he was wearing armor, then realized he was just very broad chested and tall. In fact, he was the largest man he'd seen since they had arrived in this world. Big Man said something calmly to the man who was pushing the girl.

Half naked guy snapped what sounded like a scornful reply, then made a gasping sound and abruptly stopped walking as he reached the door. The large man said something else very calmly and took the girl by the arm and half-naked man let her go.

Big Man pulled the girl gently inside and it was then that John could see that the man's other hand was buried in half-naked guy's crotch. He released his grip at that moment and the smaller man dropped to the ground, immediately curling up in a ball groaning pitifully.

The lieutenant watched as the guard walked over and said something to the man on the ground, when he felt a tug on his shoulder.

Turning he saw Murphy mouth, "What the hell is going on in there?" then he quickly added, "Sir."

Pontus gave him a steadying clap on the shoulder and motioned that they should move back down the hill. Once there he gave the private a brief play by play recap of the action then said, "Let's get back to the group."

Chapter 26: The Bunker

Dr. Stone arrived at the medical supply tent in Camp Nowhere, the site of his little archeological dig. He saw a single guard standing outside the tent.

"Good morning sir," the private greeted him.

"Good morning. How are things proceeding?" Stone asked.

"Very well sir," then with a hushed voice, "Dougherty has been down in the hole for about two hours."

This brought a nod from the doctor and he entered the tent.

Stone hadn't been in the best shape when he'd gone back into active duty, but the past few weeks of hiking back and forth between the village and the military camp, and of course the digging, had considerably increased his endurance and cardiovascular conditioning.

Progress on excavating the underground bunker was taking too long. It was just a question of time, he had to spend a lot of his time in the village, especially given the recent activity. He had many wounded prisoners to attend to.

Dr. Stone had requested a non-rotating guard duty for the medical supply tent. He wanted to have "people I can hold accountable day after day", he'd told the colonel. He knew that would get him the most junior least skilled men, as was his wish. After getting to know the two daytime guards he had recruited them to his cause with nothing more than a promise of something better coming and a vague mention that he might be able to find a way back to their own time.

Then he had risked bringing them further into his confidence so they could assist in removing dirt from the bunker. He openly told the men he was testing them, their loyalty and reliability.

He'd told his two recruits Privates Dougherty and Worthy, both draftees, to proceed cautiously and to quickly put any bodies discovered into body bags lest the smell reveal their little mining operation. He'd also come up with the clever idea to put the removed dirt into sandbags and had the men line the outside of the tent with them.

It was funny what you could hide in plain sight. Everyone was busy so they couldn't bother to check on what everyone else was doing. The only person in the whole camp that would question the doctor's activities would be Colonel Erickson, but he had so many other issues to worry about that Stone didn't think he'd get around to it. And if he did, Stone had an explanation ready.

The first body Dr. Stone had discovered had been well preserved, but quickly began to decay once uncovered. He'd had to dispose of it quickly and did so *piecemeal*. He was better prepared for the next one, also a soldier. Both men appeared to have died of asphyxiation and showed signs of having ingested dirt.

The most recent body that had been found had also been the first interesting one. He appeared to be a civilian, possibly a lab technician or scientist based on his clothing, and had been discovered seated at a table covered with electronic equipment.

Dr. Stone made his way to the back of the tent, around piles of boxes, to where the underground bunker was exposed and illuminated from within. He crawled down a ladder into the first room of the bunker, which was round like its elevated roof.

The dirty face of Private Dougherty turned to face him, "Good morning sir."

Stone looked around, noticing a lot of progress since last he'd been here three days before, "You men have been busy."

"Yes sir, after we heard about that engagement in the village a couple days ago, I figured you wouldn't be able to break away for a while, so we wanted to get as much done as possible before you returned," the private said proudly.

Ah, it was nice to have employees that aimed to please. "Impressive Private."

"Let me show you..." the private said motioning over to the far wall which was made of concrete. "There's a wire bundle coming through the wall here. It goes out into a heavy duty pipe, looks like it's shielded. The bundle itself," the young man said gripping the inches thick group of cables, "has more than one power cable and looks like multiple data lines."

"You seem to know your cables Private," the doctor said, curious.

Dougherty smiled, "Yeah, I did computer IT work back home."

Dr. Stone looked it over and agreed with the assessment.

"Very interesting," he said. "Keep up the steady work, don't worry too much about speed. Thoroughness, care and secrecy are more important. I'm trusting you, don't let anyone know what you find, there could be something down here that would cause unrest in the unit, and we don't want any more of that than we already have."

"Yes sir. Me and Worthy have been mostly keeping to ourselves," he asserted. After a pause he said, "Sir, do you really think there could be something down here that could help us get back home?"

The doctor answered carefully, "It could very well be Private. But if not, take comfort in the fact that this is important work and will help us to further ourselves in this present time. I'm sure there are much better places to see and live in than this valley."

Chapter 27: Construction

Colonel Erickson looked around him at four partially constructed buildings, two had a complete framework and two others had only just begun. He surveyed the work and thought, *Finally, we are making progress.*

On this large plateau, which overlooked Camp Nowhere in the valley below, the men and women of his unit had been clearing trees and brush in earnest for the past ten days. The harvested trunks and large branches had been fashioned into building materials, the product of which he was looking at now. The priority was to build barracks so they could begin moving people out of the tents they had been living in for over a month into something with more space and permanence.

His soldiers had named the new site *Fort Somewhere*.

Satisfied with what he saw, Erickson walked over and sat at his table that was setup under an awning next to a Bradley armored vehicle. As he sat at the table he lifted a cellphone that was being used as a paperweight, someone's idea of a joke, and opened the folder containing the scouting report regarding the Warlord's Fort. He had gone over them in detail with the scouting party when they had returned, asking lots of questions and looking at printouts of the pictures they had taken. It had been on the back burner since then with so much else to do. But now it was time to revisit the matter.

As he looked at the pictures of the buildings in the compound the one on the far side stood out to him. Though the size was roughly the same as the four barracks buildings, the similarities stopped there. The roof was short in height and had a statue of some type of animal atop it. The body was rounded across the top and sides, some of his people suggested it was some kind of livestock, but that didn't make sense to the colonel. Viewing the picture on the computer in its highest resolution and trying some different image enhancing features in the software provided a bit more detail and the colonel was looking at hardcopies of those images now. The animal statue was four legged, and the body was the shape of, perhaps a hippo.

As he continued looking at it, he noticed a man walking toward him. The colonel didn't know the man by sight, but assumed it was the man he had been waiting for.

As the specialist got closer he spoke, "Colonel, I was told to report to you here?" he said hesitantly, like he thought he was in trouble.

"Yes, have a seat Specialist Wu," the man's name on his uniform confirmed it. "I asked for whoever in the unit had the most knowledge of Korean or Chinese traditions, culture, history, and so on... I'm told that is you."

The young man looked relieved and as he sat down said, "Yes sir, well I know a little."

"We have some pictures of an encampment about 20 kilometers from the village. Most of their buildings are plain, but I'm trying to identify the figure on top of this one." The colonel spun the picture around so the young man could see it. "We're just trying to learn as much as we can about them. Most of the warriors that were killed during the attack on the village had this same snake design on their arm, this looks different though." Colonel Erickson pulled another picture which showed the forearm of one of the deceased.

Looking at the picture of the tattooed arm the young man said, "Huh, that doesn't look like much to me. I think a snake is as good a guess as any."

The colonel moved back to the first picture, "What about this thing on top of the building. Kind of looks like a cow or hippo to me. But it's like someone is riding it."

Specialist Wu looked and said, "Hmm... ah, I think this is supposed to be Xuán Wǔ, the Black Tortoise. It's symbolic of a Chinese constellation, represents North and something else," he turned the picture back toward the colonel. "See here is the shell and head, and this that you thought might be a rider is actually a snake. There is a legend about a man that becomes a god, and in the process he shed all the evil from his body, which created the tortoise and the snake."

"I only know a little of the mythology behind it and I might not have it completely right," he shook his head apologetically. "It's stuff from when I was a kid."

Colonel Erickson smiled, "No, that's helpful. It's more than I had five minutes ago. Is there anything else you can think of?"

"Another name for it is the Black Warrior of the North. These Warlord's troops dress in all black so that might be why," Wu paused. "I can't think of anything else that might be useful in regards to the symbolism or story behind it," he concluded.

"Do you speak any foreign languages Specialist?" the colonel asked.

"Yes sir, I'm pretty fluent in Mandarin Chinese, at least speaking it. Not as good at reading and writing it," the young man replied.

The colonel spoke, "Okay, well thanks for your time Specialist. I might ask for your assistance again if we get more information, I'll let you know. You're dismissed," the colonel said pleasantly.

Wu stood, "Yes, sir," and turned to leave. Then he paused, "Sir, can I ask you a question?"

The colonel could tell from the young man's tone that this wasn't going to be a military matter. He shifted his mindset subtly, "Sure go ahead."

"Do you really think that we'll never see our families again?" the sorrow in his slender face was measurable.

Erickson exhaled and said, "I haven't seen any reason to think we will. Whatever has happened to us, it seems real and beyond our control. I'm sorry I wish I could offer you some reason to hope otherwise." Then he added, "But we're going to be keeping busy around here and eventually I think we'll adjust. The people in the village we met are friendly. These warriors are another matter, but we'll just have to go a day at a time for now."

Wu nodded lightly, and looked resigned, "Thank you for being straight with me sir."

Colonel Erickson was worried that more and more of the men would feel the hopelessness he saw now on this man's face. He had to do something to turn it around. Building permanent shelters was a good start but there needed to be more, everyone had to have something to do and something to look forward to.

Chapter 28: Listen to Mother

John sat outside of Meishan's small house in the warm afternoon sun, waiting for her and the others to come outside. The last three weeks, since returning from the scouting mission to the Warlord's fort, had all led to this point.

For most of that time the lieutenant had been leading another construction project, building a barracks at Fort Somewhere, which was up on the plateau overlooking Camp Nowhere. The work had been slow going thanks to rain, but he and his crew had done the best that they could. At least rain was a good incentive to get a roof up. Unfortunately rain also made things quite slippery and John had taken a hard fall, badly bruising his left arm.

Dr. Stone recommended that he be taken off of construction for a minimum of one week and get some rest. Besides just dealing with the pain and stiffness of the injury it also meant that he was going to miss the second reconnaissance trip to the Warlord's fort which was really disappointing.

John had protested to Colonel Erickson but he had agreed with Dr. Stone that John should rest. Then John's boss, Captain Pearce, said he would step in to take his place leading the recon team which had set his mind at ease. Then the colonel had given John a carrot, permission to be away from base for a couple of days.

After that had sunk in, he had seized on an idea. With the help of one of the village interpreters, he had asked Meishan to come with him on what would essentially be a hike and campout. Her face had lit up with the idea.

He and Meishan would set out the next morning, but first John wanted to make sure that she was better dressed for the activity. So he had borrowed, actually bartered, some clothes from one of the female soldiers in the unit, basics like pants, tank top, shirt and, most importantly, boots. PFC Nancy Joiner had also been kind enough to come with him today to give the items to Meishan and help her get acquainted with them.

John heard the door and Meishan's mother, Ping, came out to join him. He stood and smiled politely then she motioned for him to sit back down.

Ping started talking. John's vocabulary had continued to grow, but there was still a lot he couldn't make out. She seemed to be talking about the village, the people, her living there. When she mentioned Meishan, John's ears perked up and he focused best he could.

She talked about Meishan as a child, probably the same kinds of stories every mom tells about her children.

Then Ping said something like, "Meishan like you."

John smiled and tried to act humble and polite, "I like Meishan, like talk to her."

He must have said it right as Ping smiled. Then she looked thoughtful and said something about Meishan's father, if John understood correctly. She seemed a little sad, but also like she was recalling happy memories.

John took a chance, "Where Meishan's father?" but was pretty sure he knew the answer.

Ping smiled and replied simply, "He sleeps," and John understood.

Then Ping looked him in the eyes and said something like, "You remember Meishan's father." It was a statement, not a question. John struggled to understand.

"You be like him," she said.

Then he got it, he reminded Ping of Meishan's father, her departed husband. Perhaps he had a similar manner or way of acting.

John took this as a complement and said, "Thank you," in her language.

Ping looked at him with happiness.

He heard the squeaking of the primitive rope hinged door again and this time Private Joiner and Meishan appeared together.

153

They looked a bit like bookends, being of the same height and build and now wearing similar clothes.

"She's all set Lieutenant, everything fits her well and I think she likes them," Nancy said.

"Thanks Joiner, I appreciate your time," he replied.

"You're welcome sir. But I will be expecting that payment we discussed," she said.

Food had become the most favored currency of the soldiers. Rations of any kind of meat were top choice, followed by any remaining delicacies that they had brought with them, such as chocolate.

Pontus handed the private a slip of paper which was essentially an IOU laundry list of items. Besides food it listed batteries and fuel which were also hot commodities.

"Yes ma'am," he said jokingly.

Meishan turned to Nancy and said in English, "Thank you." Then she turned to John.

John smiled and said in Okor, "I come tomorrow morning."

John left soon after and headed to Shanty Town for the night. He hadn't looked forward to anything in a long time, not since they had arrived in this place about two months before. It was a nice feeling, it was almost… normal.

Chapter 29: R is for Recon

Private First Class Matthew Murphy looked up at the sun that beat on them mercilessly and wiped his forehead with a sleeve. He thought back to how cold and rainy it had been for the better part of two weeks until yesterday, when it seemed that summer had finally come.

As he came upon a large tree, he paused and allowed himself to stretch to his full height, which felt great as he had been walking crouched most of the day.

Murphy couldn't believe it but he really *felt* like a soldier now. When they had invaded North Korea just a couple of months before, he'd felt scared and awkward. His brief taste of combat and then the first recon mission had initiated him into the fraternity. He'd never aspired to be a soldier but had to admit that for the first time in his life he really felt like a man.

Private Murphy and nine other men were on this recon mission, which was essentially a repeat of the one he had gone on three weeks earlier with Lt. Pontus. But this time the patrol was being led by Captain Pearce the commanding officer of E Troop. Except for Lt. Pontus all the members of the original patrol were present, including Corporal Jenkins. Ever since his friend and scout partner Jones had been injured, Matt had been paired up with Rodney Jenkins. He liked Rod because he was funny in a subtle way and got along well with everyone.

Matt had never spoken to the captain before yesterday. That was when word had come that they were definitely going out on another reconnaissance mission to the fort. It had been discussed off and on since they had returned from the first trip but now it was in motion.

The team had headed out right after sun up. The plan was to take their sweet time and get to the fort after dark so they could do some stealthy poking around. Then move on to the nearby settlement before sunrise and see what was there and what the people were like.

The boy from the village would be instrumental in going into the town, since he could blend in. Kuson said they knew of the town in question, but hadn't had contact with them in many seasons. And he was surprised to hear about the fort.

Besides Captain Pearce one of the other newcomers to the group was Specialist George Wu. He was also going to be part of the town snooping since he could pass for a local, at least visually. He was assigned to the Regimental Headquarters section and normally wouldn't be out scouting, his was a support role and he seemed a bit nervous traipsing through the woods.

The group soon reached the vicinity of the small base camp where Lt. Pontus had taken a guy down with a knife. That had been an intense few minutes. Captain Pearce sent Turner and Jenkins to check out the camp, the rest of the group just found good concealment and took a breather.

After about 15 minutes the scouts returned. Murphy crouched near the captain along with the rest of the team.

"No activity in the camp, its dead," the sergeant said, "I can't say whether or not they've been back there since we last went through, but if they did, doesn't look like they took anything, or left anything."

Captain Pearce seemed pleased at this and told them it was time to get on the move again.

* * *

When the injury to his arm had occurred Lt. Pontus hadn't thought of it as a good thing, far from it. His immediate thoughts had been obscenity laced, but had managed to just yell out in pain. After the doctor's assessment he had been mad that he couldn't continue with the building project and then realized he was going to miss the recon mission.

But now as he walked alongside Meishan in the summer sun, the phrase "blessing in disguise" came to mind. He hadn't realized how stressful the time had been since their arrival in this world. He'd seen combat on two occasions and had subdued and knifed, killed, a man. Images of all of those situations, and faces, came back to him again and again whether he was awake or asleep.

John and Meishan had departed the village early in the morning for a hike up into the foothills. He figured they'd just go for a couple of hours and see where they ended up. He was really looking forward to spending the day with Meishan. The most time they'd had alone before this had been two hours.

Now they had lots of time and nothing but the beautiful countryside to distract them. They walked mostly in silence because it was too hard for them to communicate and make progress in their walk at the same time. They stopped on occasion to rest, but really it was to have the chance to talk. John didn't need a break and he had been impressed with Meishan's pace up into the hills.

John had a large field pack with food, water, clothes, shelter and other essentials for the journey and also wore a Beretta pistol on his hip. He had given Meishan her own small pack to bring what she wanted and he had put extra water and food in it.

They had been hiking for about three hours, heading roughly southeast. John mostly led the way through the trees and brush, but occasionally Meishan took point as was the case now. It was a little strange seeing her in these regular, modern clothes. She seemed to like them, perhaps she was even proud of them but he decided that he liked how she looked in her own clothing. He liked that she was different.

As they crested another ridge, the trees thinned out quite a bit, perhaps from fire or just erosion, John thought. There was a good view to the east and John thought this was as good a place as any to setup camp.

John dropped his pack and indicated with a thumbs-up to Meishan that he thought this was a good place to stop for the day.

She had quickly learned the thumbs-up signal and they used it frequently.

He had her watch as he setup the tent but she had soon joined in, fascinated with the material, the nylon, it was made of. It was a small simple tent and setup in a few minutes.

For the rest of the afternoon they just sat, talked, and wandered around the hill they were on, taking in the view.

Chapter 30: The Perfect Night

The evening was warm but comfortable. John Pontus lay on the ground looking at the darkening sky. Nearby the campfire was crackling and John was just enjoying the moment. It had been a fun day, the most pleasant he could recall.

Talking with Meishan was becoming easier. They had learned each other's facial expressions, gestures and more vocabulary. The two were also developing their own language, borrowing phrases from both Okor and English and even adding in some words of their own.

John heard soft footsteps approaching from behind him as he continued to look out toward the horizon where the moon was just peeking up from behind a not too distant mountain. Then the shadowy figure of Meishan came and knelt down next to him.

In the faint fire light he saw that she had changed her clothes and was wearing the pretty delicate dress she had worn on their previous dates. He looked up at her face, admiring the craftsmanship of her features.

She scooted closer and lay down next to him. He pulled her in, his left arm wrapped around her shoulders, and she rested her head on his chest.

With his other hand he reached over and stroked her smooth black hair, enjoying how it felt between his fingers. For a long time they laid in that embrace.

She broke the moment leaning up on her elbow and turning her head to look down at him. The flickering firelight danced in her hazel eyes as she stared passionately at him.

The world slowed and John experienced every moment distinctly. She leaned down and pressed her lips against his. The kiss became kisses and he lost all sense of time. Occasionally they paused to breathe and look into each other's eyes. John ran his hand along the smooth fabric of her dress to her side, her waist, her hips, her thighs. He could hear her breathing quicken as he caressed her.

They continued like this for an unbounded time, then she laid her head back down on his chest and he wrapped both of his arms around her feeling content and relaxed. It seemed they had all the time in the world to enjoy one another, there was no rush.

When he had been a teenager he had always been anxious around girls. Then on the occasion he was able to be alone with one he liked, he tended to push the physicality, not really enjoying the steps along the way. There was *one* goal, and he had been driven toward it.

Now, here was this young woman who likely had never even kissed a man prior to himself. She was innocent and untainted by the life that he had known growing up. He cherished that about her and hoped that nothing, including his own actions, would change that.

The night was almost windless and as John laid there holding this beautiful woman, he looked again to the horizon. The full moon was now fully exposed above the dark outline of the mountains and looked enormous. It hung silent, still and bright. This was the most beautiful sight he had ever seen. The most perfect night of his life and nothing could make it better.

* * *

Private Murphy was bored. He and the patrol had reached the area of the Warlord's fort in the late afternoon and carefully probed the surrounding area not finding anyone. Then they had laid low waiting for dark.

But even after the sun had gone down the full moon had lit the ground with amazing brightness. So the captain said they were going to wait several more hours until the moon was obscured by mountains and trees. In the meantime they just waited and rehearsed their plans.

The idea was to split into teams of two. One team would move around the right side of the fort to the east, so they could get another look at the military camp to see if anything had changed. Since Murphy was the only one in the group that had seen it the last time he was designated to go there along with the captain.

Team two, Corporal Jenkins and Specialist Wu, were to go after the big prize. They would try to gain entry into the compound and get a look inside the curious building with the turtle on the roof. It was risky, during the day they had seen guards posted by this building and the guard tower always had at least two warriors in it, so they were going to take it slow and careful.

Then Murphy's boredom was interrupted by Captain Pearce's hushed voice, "Okay men, the moon will be down soon, let's get started."

Jenkins crouch walked towards a tree where he was to setup a remote video camera with a view over the wall. Murphy watched him scamper up the tree barefoot and disappear among the leaves. But a minute later he heard a hollow sounding *clack* noise. In the next moment the branches shook and Jenkins suddenly dropped to the ground, a fall of at least six feet.

Murphy tried to balance quickness with stealth as he scampered over to check on his friend. By the fading moonlight he could see Jenkins' face contorted in pain. He looked up at Murphy and said, "First I dropped the damn camera. Then I just slipped off the limb, it's so wet!"

A few others gathered near the fallen private, including Captain Pearce who asked, "Can you walk?"

Jenkins tried to put weight on his injured left foot, and grimaced in pain.

The captain said, "Okay, you're not going to be walking anytime soon, but we should try and get your boot on before that foot swells up."

Sergeant Turner found and picked up the camera, "Power knob is popped off. It's done. We'll need plan B for a lookout."

They got Jenkins' boot on despite the pain and quietly dragged him farther away from the fort.

The captain said, "Okay Jenkins, you sit tight and keep your foot up." Then to the rest of the group, "I need someone to sub for him to go look at that turtle building. It's the top item on the colonel's wish list."

Murphy thought that the captain was talking right to him and he felt like it was his duty to cover the detail for his friend, "I can do it Captain."

"Okay Private, you've got it. You and Wu start working your way around and get into position. Wait for the moon to be fully obscured before you try anything," the captain said.

Private Murphy met with Jenkins and Wu to talk about the mission and what they'd planned to do. Then, he and Wu slowly made their way around the left side of the fort, well inside the tree line. Once near their intended position, they laid low and waited for it to get darker.

At first the mission hadn't seemed too difficult, just find a way inside the outer wall to look at the building and see what was inside. Now that he was looking at the ten foot high fence Matt Murphy was thinking, *You want me to do what?*

The physical part wouldn't be tough. He'd just throw a line up over the top of the fence, climb it, drop another line down the other side and scoot down. Wu would follow and together they'd investigate. Getting back out would be just as simple.

But everything in between was risky. When it had still been daylight, two guards had been seen standing in front of the building they wanted to investigate. Even if they didn't routinely walk the perimeter of the building they'd sure as hell come looking if they heard something. Matt hoped that they didn't stand the post at night.

The moon was finally dipping below the tops of the tallest nearby trees. Murphy shook the sleepiness from his head and as he imagined climbing over the wall his adrenalin started to pump. He and Wu put all of their unnecessary gear in a pile, including their cumbersome and potentially noisy helmets.

Two more minutes and the ground before them grew noticeably darker. Matt slowly moved out of the bushes and duck walked, out in the open, toward the corner of the tall wall, with Wu right behind him. Matt hoped that the angle they were approaching from would prevent the guards in the distant watch tower from seeing them.

Halfway there, Murphy thought.

He held tightly to the only item he was carrying, a silenced MP5 sub machinegun. Behind him, George Wu had a pack with their climbing gear and Sergeant Turner's digital Nikon, but no weapon, save a knife. Their plan was light, quick and quiet.

They reached the base of the wall without incident. Private Murphy retrieved the first climbing rope and hook from Wu's bag. He uncoiled it, hefted the hook and, with his back to the wall, gave it a smooth toss up over his head.

The hook cleared the top of the wall and the rope went taught, with Wu holding it. He slowly pulled back and Murphy saw it was holding firm. Murphy took Wu's backpack then slung his sub-gun as well. He took hold of the rope and climbed, hand over hand with his legs loosely wrapped around the rope.

It took less than a minute to ascend the wall. Matt peeked over the top focusing on the guard tower, about 300 feet away. He couldn't see anyone in it, so he hoped that meant they didn't see him either. Checking the dark ground inside the wall he couldn't see anyone there either.

He threw a leg up and over carefully straddling the fence between two of the large wooden pilings. Retrieving a second rope from the bag, he laid the hook over the outside of the wall and let the rope fall to the ground inside the fort. He tugged on it with his hand and felt the hook grab.

He motioned for George to come up and within a minute they were both on the ground inside the wall of the fort. They quickly moved behind the target building, only ten feet away, then took a minute to catch their breath.

Murphy produced night vision goggles from the back pack and strapped them to his head. Everything was still dim, but it was a bright green dim instead of a dark black dim. Peeking around the corner to the side of the building, he didn't see a guard, but there was a glow coming from around the front of the building. On the side of the building was a large door, perhaps 20 feet wide and as tall as the wall of the building, about eight feet.

Murphy crept along the wall the short distance to the door. It looked more like a barn door than anything else, *a stable?* There wasn't any obvious way of opening it, and Murphy couldn't even see how it opened as he looked in vain for a pivot point or similar mechanism. He reached out to feel the edge which was sticking out about an inch from the wall. Giving it a slight push, then pull, it felt solidly in place.

Retreating back around the corner to the back of the building, he whispered to Wu, "We're not getting in that way."

Instead they moved along the back wall of the building and soon Matt saw a person sized door about halfway down. Approaching it Murphy saw a handle clearly sticking out of one side.

Turning to look at Wu, Murphy gave him a nod and they prepared to see if the door would open, his heart pounding.

Matt gave the handle a try, a light push and it opened easily. The inside was lit from somewhere, though not very brightly. As the door opened more Matt saw a hallway lead out to a larger room where a single gas lantern was hanging from a metal fixture.

Murphy removed his night vision goggles and entered the hall with Wu right behind him quietly closing the door. As he did Murphy saw a large wooden box that had been sitting behind the door. He gave the top a tug, and the lid lifted off. Matt was overcome with the strange expectation that he would find coins or some other item of value, but the crate was empty.

Walking down the hall toward the middle of the building Matt saw many more crates of varying sizes, some open, some closed and some with piles of rags lying atop them. As they got to the middle of the room Matt saw that to the left and right of the hall there were large fabric curtains extending eight or ten feet then a wooden wall went another ten or so to the far wall of the building.

Reaching up to the nearest curtain, Matt's anticipation spiked. He tugged the thick material to one side and as light spilled into the chamber behind he saw... *nothing.* It was just an empty room, with a box here and there. But there was something familiar about the smell in the room, it was stale and grimy but he couldn't quite place it.

A little disappointed, he scanned the rest of the interior. The building was mostly taken up by these curtained off chambers, a total of four of them. He needed to check all four. If they were all empty, then he'd take the time to scrutinize them more closely.

Reaching up to pull open the next curtain he kind of expected the room to be empty. Opening it a few inches he saw this one had something within, something large and dark. Matt pulled the curtain further to get more light inside.

He struggled with recognition as he studied the large mound. *Strange looking,* was his initial assessment. Then his eyes looked down at the floor and... his heart nearly stopped from shock.

"Oh shit! Wu this is a," his words were interrupted by a dull clang, like a metal bat hitting a baseball. Matt spun around just in time to see George falling to the floor, and a man swinging something down at him.

Murphy tried to bring his gun up to fire, or at least intercept the object arcing down at his skull, but he wasn't quick enough. His gun quietly fired two rounds into the wall as the blow glanced off the side of his head. The pain came on strong increasing with every second.

Matt fell hard to the floor, both hands cradling his head. He couldn't see, couldn't open his eyes from the pain, then felt consciousness fading.

His final thought was... *Black Tortoise.*

Chapter 31: Captured

Through the agonizing pain in his head, the only thing Private Murphy could think was, *I'm not dead?*

But he wasn't sure if that situation was going to change. His head must be injured pretty badly, and... he could barely stand the pain, it even hurt to think.

Matt tried opening his eyes. The room, or wherever he was, was agreeably dark. The only light he could see was a small sliver on the floor a couple feet in front of him. Even that faint light was enough for Matt to realize he couldn't focus his eyes well, looking at his bare feet stretched out in front of him, he saw four silhouettes instead of two.

He tried to rub his face but his hands wouldn't obey. He wondered for a scary moment if he was paralyzed, but then he felt the pain of something tight around his wrists and decided it was more likely he was just tied up.

Closing his eyes again, he felt himself drifting off and his mind wandered.

What is that smell?

Musky... he thought as he drifted in and out of consciousness.

Sleepy.

Then in a moment of clarity Murphy thought, *there's a leak in the tent.*

As beautiful as it was, that was one big drawback of camping in the Seattle area. Even in the summer rain wasn't unusual, just unwelcome. Especially up in the Cascade Mountains, where it got down right cold at night even in July.

The water on his face grew from a drip to a trickle and then to a deluge, shocking Private Murphy awake. He opened his eyes and looked around in confusion, then the pain in his head came roaring back.

"Ahhhh!"

He was in a small room and light was coming in from the open door in front of him. The light was partially obscured by a large person standing there. The man was holding a standard army helmet that Matt realized had just been used to douse him with water.

The man said something to someone outside the room, in what Matt assumed was Okor.

Matt glanced around the room and saw that it was a living space for someone. Across from him was a bed mat that didn't look terribly comfortable, but his butt told him that it would be much better than the wood floor he was sitting on.

After the initial surge had subsided, he realized that his head wasn't hurting as much as it had been before, but his wrists were very sore where the rope or cord was wound around them and he couldn't feel his hands. He tried to shift but with his feet also bound, he could barely move at all.

A second man entered the room dressed in black armor, but of a different kind than Matt had seen others wear, the texture was smooth and well crafted. He was wearing a helmet and a mask covered the lower part of his face and chin. It looked like a costume piece.

This man, quite a bit smaller than the other, said something to the big man and he produced a knife, Matt thought it was probably his own. He leaned down and cut the rope that bound his feet. Then he pulled Matt's head down and cut the rope from his hands as well. The relief in his wrists was quickly replaced with a burning sensation as circulation returned to his hands.

The big guy then led him to the bed mat and indicated he should sit. The second man, clearly in charge, produced a wooden cup and handed it to Murphy. He took it, painful as that simple act was, and took a sip of, water he was thankful to realize.

The boss started talking calmly even pleasantly Matt thought. Then he said something that sounded like a question. Matt looked at him blankly and said, "Uh, I don't understand what you're saying." The man in turn looked blankly at him. Clearly he didn't understand Matt either.

The man in charge spoke once again, this time saying only one word, "Zhu" tapping his chest.

Okay, that must be his name, Matt thought. He replied, "Murphy."

The man nodded, "Muf-fee," and then a string of words Matt couldn't understand.

The private didn't know if this was going to be a good thing or a bad thing. He couldn't tell them anything even if he wanted to. He wondered how long it would take for this man to realize that.

"I'm sorry, I don't understand you," Matt said calmly.

Zhu again spoke asking unknown questions and Matt started to get a little scared.

After another minute of Matt not responding the good cop was visibly upset and it was bad cop's turn. The big man stepped forward and struck him across the face with a piece of thick leather, it stung badly.

"Ahh!" Matt more exhaled than said.

The large man hit him again and again. Matt's cheeks felt like they were on fire, making him temporarily forget the pain in his head. He tried not to yell out, thinking it would make them mad for some reason. Matt knew that he was supposed to be tough, that he wasn't supposed to cooperate, but the truth was he couldn't understand them and he wanted them to believe that.

"I can't understand you. I don't know what you are saying," he implored them.

The big man just looked down at him remorselessly, then looked to the man in charge. From behind the mask, the man seemed to calm down. Then he said something else, but this time in a different language. Matt still couldn't understand it but there was something familiar about it. He just looked at the man quizzically and said, "I can't understand you."

Something on Matt's face must have made an impression because he thought he saw the man smile. He said something else, this time in Okor, and he sounded apologetic, or somber. He reached into a pouch, and pulled out a small chain. He stepped forward and handed it to Matt.

Private Murphy looked at the chain and saw immediately that it was a set of dog tags, the military identification that all soldiers wore. He read the name, Specialist George Wu. He realized then that he must be dead. This was part of being a real soldier that Murphy wished had never come. He slipped Wu's dog tags over his head right next to his own so he wouldn't lose them.

The big man tied his arms together again, but this time in front of him. He said something and even though Matt couldn't understand his words, he got the message perfectly well. They were going to allow him a small measure of comfort, but he was to behave himself or else.

Matt nodded and said in return, "I understand," but he also knew that he needed to get out and warn his team about the dangers concealed within this fort.

Chapter 32: aka Rahab

It had been several hours since Murphy's meeting with the man in charge and the guy who looked like a bouncer. The sun had gone down and there was barely any light filtering into his tiny windowless room. He just sat on the bed, hands bound in front of him, and thought about what he should do.

What he had seen in that building the night before seemed like a dream, and with his head injury, which still throbbed, he wasn't sure if it was real or not. It seemed real, but the image of a giant sleeping turtle made him question if it was all just a delusion.

In the past few hours he'd heard a number of people coming and going in the hall outside his room, men's voices, women's voices. Most sounding pleasant others even playful. Then, in the room next to him he had heard the unmistakable sounds of a man and woman enjoying each other's company in embarrassing detail.

Matt remembered the scene that Lt. Pontus described on their first recon of this base. The crying woman running out into the night. Whatever else this building was used for, part of it seemed to be a brothel, or something worse.

Things were quiet now, he heard occasional heavy footsteps plodding up and down the hall but no voices and no more visitors.

The footsteps were back again, and they seemed to stop outside his door. Private Murphy tensed as he waited, then the door opened. The shadowy but unmistakable figure of the big man filled the doorway.

The man entered the room and closed the door behind him. He approached Matt, leaned down and pulled some strands of the rope around his wrists and the binding dropped to the floor. Then he motioned for Matt to be quiet.

He helped Matt to his feet and led him to the door, where he cocked his ear and listened. Then he opened the door slightly, peering out. After a moment, he pulled Matt gently out into the hall with him.

With urgency on his face the man pointed Matt down the hallway to the left which went perhaps 30 feet into darkness ending in a wall. The big man pointed down the hall, and then exaggeratedly hooked his hand to the left.

Murphy realized that this man was helping him to escape. Again the man thrust his arm down the hall and pushed Matt. He shook off his shock and began walking down the hall, the wooden floor smooth on his bare feet. Then he quickened into a jog. As he reached the end of the hall, he looked left and there was a doorway, slightly ajar.

As he started to move toward the door he looked back from where he had come and saw the large man throw himself headfirst into the wall and then heard him shout. Now Matt felt like he'd just been set up.

Why all the drama? Just freaking kill me already.

Then an arm reached out from the dark doorway ahead and pulled him inside, Matt didn't resist. Once inside, by the dim flame of a lantern, he saw the figure of a woman dressed in a silky robe. She said something with a quiet intensity and pulled him further into the room, closer to the light.

The woman was perhaps his age or younger, and looked a lot like the women of the village. She was small and slim and her hair was short and black.

She pushed him down onto a bed mat and started to tug on his waist band, all the while speaking that same hushed but insistent tone that he couldn't understand a word of. Matt wasn't sure what was happening, but had the sense that she was trying to help him.

He complied with her direction, removing his camouflaged pants which she took and stuffed under a sheet, leaving him in his underwear. Then she laid him flat on the mat and, pulling up her robe, straddled him. The whole thing seemed a bit surreal and he wondered if he was having a delusion.

171

Matt heard a commotion growing outside the room, voices shouting and footsteps running.

She slipped the top of her robe down revealing petite breasts, her skin a radiant bronze in the faint light. Then she started to raise herself up and down on top of him while moaning loudly. Matt felt himself both aroused and flushed from embarrassment at the same time.

A moment later the door burst open, and he heard loud voices shout into the room. The woman on top of him jerked in mock surprise and screeched. She turned to face the intruders and said something to them in a harsh, scolding tone.

One of the men said something apologetically and promptly left the room, closing the door behind him.

The young woman returned to her feigned sexual activity, though a bit less energetic than before and glanced over her shoulder at the door. It was then that Matt noticed something else about her bare chest. Just below her collar bone was a black tattoo a few inches long. It was the same style snake that he had seen branded onto the arms of many of the warriors.

Suddenly she stopped moving, leapt to her feet and covered herself. She spoke insistently to Matt and pulled him to his feet, leading him to the back wall of her room. She picked up a small metal rod and started prying on one of the roughhewn logs that made up the wall, which to Matt's surprise pulled away revealing a narrow gap.

She looked up at him and pointed to the gap, indicating that he should go in. This was all happening so fast that Matt hesitated. In a quiet but insistent tone she ordered him to go through. He did as he was told, crawling hands first into the dark void.

He couldn't see anything but darkness in the area he was entering. He felt the ground was dirt, but the air was stale and still, so he didn't think he was outside. The hole he was crawling through was tight around his waist, but he shimmied his way through, then tumbled to the ground.

He righted himself and looked back from where he had come. The woman shoved his wadded up pants through the hole, then said something to him in a soft, pleasant tone. Then the log got pushed back into place, closing the hole and casting Matt once again into total darkness.

Private Murphy just sat there for a moment, processing what had happened, and belatedly thought.

Thank you.

Chapter 33: Looking Up

John Pontus woke early as the sun lit up the tent he and Meishan were sleeping in. He lay enjoying the quiet for a few serene moments. The tent soon got a little too warm and he went out into the morning where the air was cool and refreshing.

He found a bottle of water and walked away from the campsite, sitting and looking out at the valley below him, thinking. The past couple of days he'd found himself doing a lot of thinking, in particular about his future.

They were stuck in this world. The immediate danger of roving bands of hostile warriors helped to give the remains of the army regiment focus and purpose. But what next? There was no longer a United States. Who or what would they serve now?

John had focused on being a soldier for so many years, all of his adult life, but now it didn't seem to matter. He'd heard of guys that were action junkies, once they got a taste of combat that is all they wanted, like a bear that had developed a taste for humans. After his brief encounters, John knew that wasn't him. He had no problem doing the job, but didn't think he'd ever, didn't want to ever, get used to or enjoy killing people.

What did interest him was spending more time with Meishan. Maybe even spending a life with her. What else mattered in this world? What was there that *he* was needed to do. There was no higher purpose or calling that he could see.

The colonel was building a settlement back at Fort Somewhere. John thought that the men and women of the unit would embrace it because there was a lack of any other obvious choice. Despite the fact that John thought the colonel was doing the best he could, it was inevitable that not everyone would be happy with the situation. Eventually, he saw the group disbanding or worse, splitting into factions.

Would he stay and help provide leadership, and if so, to whom? There was no moral compass, nothing showing him the way to act. Part of John wanted to just strike out on his own... well hopefully not completely on his own.

Glancing over his shoulder he saw Meishan emerge from the tent, wearing her hiking clothes. She pushed back her dark tussled hair and gave him a smile as she moved to their dead fire pit and started trying to get it going.

Two nights before had been special for them. They weren't married and had only experienced the beginnings of intimate contact, but yet there was a bond that was strong. As strong as it had been with any woman John had ever known.

Yesterday they had mostly stayed near the campsite, exploring the area together. She had rarely left his side. She was playful, which was something new, and her smiles were bigger and brighter. They had shared warm embraces and a few passionate kisses.

That evening had been cool, so they stayed close to the fire, continuing to talk and share each other's space. As the evening had grown into night she had said something in her language to the effect of.

"My heart likes you."

Dismissing these pleasant memories, and all his ambiguous thoughts of the future, John stood and stretched, then walked over to greet her.

He squatted down and kissed Meishan on the cheek saying, "Good morning." She turned, replied in kind, and they shared a soft kiss on the lips.

My heart likes you very much as well, he thought.

John stood and left Meishan to tend the fire, walking again out toward the edge of the plateau. In that moment he felt... peace.

Buzzzzzz.

At first his mind dismissed the message coming in through his ears, just a noise, a common sound long remembered. Then there was confusion as his subconscious mind sent a message into his conscious mind, *Something isn't right.*

It was a buzz, distant, familiar. The droning grew louder and John finally turned to look, instinctively sweeping the skies for the source.

Even as denial was insisting *it couldn't be*, there it was... an airplane.

It was moving in his general direction at low altitude, it would pass close by. All John could say for sure at this point was that it was a small, single engine propeller aircraft. He wasn't an expert on airplanes, but did know his way around machines in general. As it drew closer he could see it had a low single wing. The nose was round and pronounced, a radial engine. It looked military in form.

John heard Meishan say something in a fearful tone and come running up, putting her arms around him. He looked down at her briefly and smiled, trying to reassure her. She looked back at him and he could see she was putting her trust in him.

Looking back to the plane he saw that its landing gear was down. *Is it going to land?* he thought. Then he realized that the landing gear struts were thick, a type that didn't fold up into the plane but stayed down all the time.

As it drew closer it angled away heading northeast. As it did so, John got a better look at its appearance which was striking. *Huh?*

On the dark green nose of the plane were painted a set of teeth, like that of a shark. He had seen pictures of military airplanes and helicopters with similar teeth painted on many times. But the design went far beyond the nose. The underside of the round tipped wings were painted to look like the wings of a giant bird, or bat, or... *dragon*?

As it passed by, he could see the visual motif was spread across the whole airplane. The landing gear had a scaly, talon-like appearance and the body of the plane had the look of a creature's body.

"A dragon?" he questioned aloud, not understanding.

As it moved off, John's last observation was of the airplane's long heavily framed canopy. He was sure that he saw two heads inside sitting in tandem.

John was almost positive that what he was looking at was a military airplane from the World War Two era. He wasn't a WWII buff, no that was his brother, but he'd had enough history at the academy and seen enough movies that he was pretty sure what he was looking at, minus the dragon disguise, was the same type of airplane that Japan had used to attack Pearl Harbor on December 7th 1941.

In that moment of realization, his future changed.

Chapter 34: It's A Rescue Mission

After realizing that Murphy and Wu had been captured, Captain Pearce had pulled his team well away from the fort. Then after the sun had come up they concealed themselves and watched as enemy patrols searched the wooded area around the fort. But they never came out far enough to be a threat.

Once night had fallen again, Captain Pearce sent a few men to gather more information about the fort and the nearby military camp down in the valley. The camp didn't have much activity, it was actually pretty quiet. The fort was similarly subdued, no change from what they had observed during the daytime.

With this information, the captain devised a plan to rescue Murphy and Wu. Since the team had just been on a scouting mission, they hadn't come prepared for an assault on prepared defenses. Instead of a full load of explosive grenades, they mostly had smoke and flash bang. They had standard M4 rifles but no light machine guns. Still Captain Pearce's assessment was that what they did have was a force multiplier, giving them an enormous advantage over their opposition. It was going to be risky, but he had no intention of leaving his men behind. While it was still dark, the captain split up his team and got them into position and waited for morning.

At last the eastern sky was starting to brighten. Pearce lay in the bushes just over one hundred meters across from the gate to the fort. With him were Sergeant Turner and Privates Camiroja and Bridgeman. His group of four was going to assault through the gate while the remaining three members of his small patrol, one of them hobbled, were spread around the perimeter of the fort to provide cover and take down targets as they appeared.

The sun had been up for several minutes before the gate started to move.

Finally, the captain thought.

Two guards appeared once the gate doors were fully open. They stood, not really at attention, but alert with their short pick axe like weapons that the captain had seen before. In the guard tower, just inside the left corner of the wall, he could see there were still just two men present.

Captain Pearce slowly lifted his M4 carbine with both hands, aiming at the left guard. A few feet away, PFC Bridgeman drew a bead on a target as well.

Just above a whisper, the captain said, "3... 2... 1... now."

As Captain Pearce said "now" he squeezed the trigger on his weapon, firing off a single shot. PFC Bridgeman did likewise. The two guards jerked oddly, their faces filled with surprise.

The captain and his three men got to their feet but did not yet leave the cover of the trees. Watching the guard tower, the captain saw the first guard's head snap to the side, followed a split second later by the reverberating crack of rifle fire.

The second guard raised his bow then fell backwards, followed by another *crack*.

"Go!" the captain yelled.

The four men sprinted toward the open gate, weapons at the ready, then they heard an explosion coming from inside the fort. As they were approaching the gate, two on either side of the opening, they heard another loud explosion, and shouts coming from inside the fort walls.

The captain slowly peered around the corner of the gate into the fort. Just about 15 meters to his left was the first of the four barracks buildings, it had a large hole on the near end and was partially on fire.

Another explosion, this time the captain could feel it and he ducked back around the corner for safety. He was still within the shrapnel zone of the grenades that Private Cushman, sitting in a tree, was launching into the enemy compound.

One more, he thought.

A few more seconds and the fourth high explosive grenade detonated, hopefully into the last of the four barracks buildings.

"Go!" Pearce shouted as he walked quickly into the fort with Private Camiroja following close behind.

The private stopped just inside the entrance and took up a seated firing position, training his rifle toward the damaged barracks buildings.

The captain, Sergeant Turner and PFC Bridgeman formed up and ran between two small buildings on their way toward the large building that was presumably the home of the warlord that they were now *at war* with.

Soon they were only ten meters from the corner of the large structure. There was a door just in from the corner and they saw a warrior lying in the dirt, his face terror stricken. He jumped to his feet once he saw them and quickly fled.

That's perfect, you all do that, the captain thought.

They arrived at the door as a group, the sergeant held a silenced sub machinegun with one hand and opened the door with his other, leading them inside.

*   *   *

Private Murphy heard the muffled sound of gunfire, then the unmistakable sound of explosions.

After being released into the narrow gap between the wall of the building and the outer wall of the fort he set out to find a way out. He wanted to get to safety, but also to link up with his comrades and warn them, but now it was too late.

After the young woman had freed him, *did that really happen,* he thought rubbing his weary eyes, he'd found his boots, socks and a small metal rod in the darkness. He'd spent hours in the dark trying to find a weak spot. Finally he'd found that at the very end of this long low hall was a simple panel covering up the end of it and he was sure he could pry it open.

The problem was that by the time he'd figured that out, it had already been daylight. It looked like it would lead right out into the courtyard, which isn't where he wanted to be while the sun was up. So he'd resigned himself to spending the day in this narrow hall waiting for sundown.

But that plan was moot now. His fellow soldiers were looking for him. He needed to meet up with them or they'd waste time trying to find him and end up getting killed or captured themselves.

Using the small rod, he started prying into the cracks of the panel. It was attached well, but he was starting to see results. It would only take a few minutes to get it off.

Then he heard a chattering sound, faint but distinct.

Too late

Chapter 35: Turtles

Private Jenkins lay just a few feet inside the tree line, with bushes on either side of him. From there he could see both the long side of the fort and the short side with the gate the other soldiers had gone through a minute before.

After he had shot both of the men in the guard tower there wasn't much else he could do to help, except watch and wait.

The young man from the village was with him, and by the look on his face was either excited or scared. *Probably both,* Jenkins thought.

About 30 meters to his right up in a tree Private Cushman was firing his Enhanced Battle Rifle over the wall at targets Jenkins couldn't see. The boom from the EBR was impressive, it had a deeper sound than the M4 he and the other soldiers were using. It fired a much larger bullet too, the 7.62mm NATO round, essentially the same as the civilian .308 Winchester cartridge popular with hunters.

Jenkins kept watch down the flanks of the fort walls. He heard short bursts of automatic fire coming from somewhere. He figured it must be Private Rockford over on the other side of the fort. His job was to discourage the warriors down in the military camp from coming up to help defend the fort.

Then suddenly, down near the end of the left side of the fort wall Jenkins saw a large wooden gate tear loose and pancake onto the ground. A split second later he saw why. Something large was moving right over the top of it, then it was obscured by a cloud of dust.

It turned toward him and as it cleared the dust he was staring at what looked like a huge turtle, at least two meters tall and wide. It had a smooth shell made up of dark plates, and a large short-necked head protruded from it the size of a rhino's.

What the...

In the next moment Jenkins saw that something wasn't right. Atop the turtle was what looked like a large snake coiled around a round metal trash can sized object, its head extended two or three feet forward. He couldn't see its feet but it was digging up an impressive amount of dirt on both sides of its body.

Through the noise of the gun fire he finally heard the sounds that pulled the mask off the monster, a metallic squeaking and the distinct sound of an internal combustion engine revving high.

Shock and disbelief gave way and he realized that what was charging toward him was a tank! It was small, but no doubt it was a tracked vehicle.

Over the din of the battle he heard a voice yelling, it was Cushman up in his tree, "There's a damn tank!"

Turning he could just barely see Cushman and yelled back, "Yeah, I know there's a tank!" But Cushman was looking into the fort, not outside of it.

There's more than one... Jenkins thought.

Next he heard machinegun fire from inside the fort. But it didn't sound like one of their M4 rifles. The rate of fire was wrong, slower, and its staccato bark had a different kind of report. It just kept firing and firing.

Down near the gate the soldiers had entered, Jenkins saw small bits of the wooden wall start to fly. It was getting chewed up in a tight area.

Cushman started firing his EBR at a high semi-automatic rate, pouring lead into something inside the fort.

The first turtle tank was now within about one hundred meters of Jenkins' position and he wondered if he was going to get overrun. Then it turned sharply, heading around toward the open gate where the team had gone in.

Jenkins switched his rifle to full-automatic mode and let loose controlled bursts into the side of the monster until his magazine was empty. But the vehicle kept moving, unfazed by the pin pricks of the small caliber weapon.

Jenkins tried to think of what else he could do. He didn't have any grenades, except smoke. Nothing that might hurt that metal beast. He couldn't see what kind of tank it was, but it was small, and moved slowly by the standards of what he was used to.

From the side of the snake wrapped turret he saw a small barrel protrude and emit flashes and he heard the chatter of machinegun fire. It was aiming up and to the side, toward where Cushman was perched in his tree.

Shit, Jenkins thought.

The young man from the village lay on the ground next to him, looking terrified. Jenkins thought about what to do next and pulled out a notepad and pencil. He hastily scribbled a note, leaving out the profanity he was thinking as it would have just taken longer to write, and handed it to the boy.

"Go to village. Give to colonel. Run fast!" he said slowly and clearly.

The boy took the note and nodded his head, then turned and scampered through the bushes for several meters. Then he stood up and ran like a gazelle, disappearing from view.

Jenkins knew that any help they could get would be far too long in coming. But he had to make sure that the rest of the unit was warned about the danger in case he and the rest of the patrol were killed or captured. Jenkins felt upside down, what seemed like a simple world had just been turned on its ear.

He heard heavy footsteps approaching. Remembering his rifle had an empty magazine he quickly drew his pistol and brought it up to meet the sound. Cushman appeared and when he saw the pistol aimed at him, he fell down awkwardly, his arms laden with two rifles.

Jenkins swore and lowered his weapon, "You okay?"

"Yeah, that freaking thing just about had me, but I cut the rope and dropped down. Nearly busted my ankle in the process," came the breathless, agitated reply. "What the hell is that thing?"

Jenkins shook his head, "I don't know, but the captain and those guys are screwed if we can't do something to stop it."

Cushman's face drew grim, "Camiroja is all F'd up man, another one of those things laid him out with M-G fire."

Jenkins nodded solemnly.

Cushman went on, "I emptied a whole mag into it, but it didn't do a damn thing. I mean, it's a tank right?"

"Yeah it's armored for sure," Jenkins replied, then he thought of something. "Look, I don't know what it is, but it sure as hell isn't one of ours. It's small and sounds old, maybe some relic from the First Korean War. Tanks that old have shit for armor in the back."

Jenkins eyed Cushman's EBR, "Try that again. Hit the sonofabitch in the back, or better yet get back into the tree and hit it from the top."

Cushman nodded, understanding, "Okay, I'll try it from down here. To hell with the damn tree."

Cushman dropped the second rifle he was carrying, an M4 with grenade launcher attached, and inserted a fresh 20 round magazine into his modified M14 battle rifle. Then he ran as fast as he could past Jenkins' position.

Jenkins knew that Cushman would get into a position where he was firing directly perpendicular to the rear of the tank, to minimize deflection. The turtle tank was stopped, just short of the open gate in the fort wall. He then had a horrible thought, *what if that fake turtle shell is armor too?*

Things were quiet inside the fort. The captain and the others were probably inside a building, which would protect them from the tank. But they had to leave sooner or later.

An ear-splitting crack rang out from Cushman's rifle. Jenkins thought the ringing in his ears was already as bad as it could get, but now that he was downrange, in front of the muzzle of the rifle, it was even worse. He quickly covered his ears before the second shot.

Jenkins couldn't see the impact or effect of the rifle fire. He knew that Cushman would hit with every shot. At just over 100 meters it would be easy for anyone to hit a big target like that and Cushman was a designated marksman.

Twenty rounds had been expended and Jenkins just watched and waited. Then he saw that the black diesel smoke coming from the back of the turtle tank had stopped. As the ringing in his ears subsided, he realized he no longer heard the engine running.

Ha, take that assholes! he thought. Then he picked up his rifle, swapped in a new 30 round magazine, switched back to semi-auto, and got it ready, training it toward the tank.

One thing that he knew about tankers, men like himself that operated in armored fighting vehicles, that was universal. None of them liked to be inside an immobilized tank, especially if it was still taking enemy fire.

"Keep hitting it," Jenkins screamed, hoping Cushman could hear him.

Unfortunately Jenkins couldn't cover his ears and hold his rifle at the same time. *Boom* went the next deafening shot and Jenkins swore to himself.

After the fourth shot Jenkins saw a hatch on the top of the tank open up. A man appeared and started to climb onto the front of the tank, *bingo*.

Jenkins estimated a three man crew on a small tank like that, maybe even two. He waited until he saw the second man emerge and fired a single shot into him. The man tumbled out of the hatch and fell to the ground. Then Jenkins switched to the first man who was still scrambling down the front slope of the turtle shell and fired at him. He couldn't tell if he had hit him or not, but he disappeared from view.

Now what?

Private Cushman came running back over, sliding down next to Jenkins.

"Good idea Corporal," the slightly younger man said, "now what?"

Rod Jenkins was still working on that, "Okay, I'll stay here, obviously, and keep an eye on that tank. You go down to the gate that it broke out of, and circle around behind the other one, see if you can knock it out too."

Pat Cushman looked hesitant.

"Yeah, I know it sucks and there could be more of those things in there. Just stay in the trees until you get around and come in from behind," he thought some more then said, "Rockford is back in that area beyond the fort. Link up with him and tell him what's going on, in case he doesn't know. Tell him to get ready to bug out, then see if you can get a shot off on that tank. But if you can't get in behind it quick and easy, pull back and we'll rendezvous back in the woods as planned."

Cushman nodded his agreement to the orders and said, "Corporal, what the hell is going on at this place? We got guys with swords, and now a tank?"

Jenkins just shook his head, "No clue man, let's just focus on getting everyone out and we'll let the officers worry about that crap, kay?"

Cushman nodded in the affirmative then turned and ran back through the trees.

Chapter 36: Heroics

After Murphy had heard the diesel engine fire up, he knew that he had failed to get out in time warn the rest of the squad. But he still needed to escape to save his own life. It took another minute or two to pry open the wood panel, what seemed like an eternity. All the while he kept hearing gunfire of all kinds outside.

Now that he had the panel free he didn't let it drop, he walked out holding it up. Peeking around the piece of wood he saw the interior security wall about 30 feet away. The large gate in the middle of the wall was still closed, but at the far end a large section of the wall was ripped open.

He didn't see any of the black armored warriors at all and, dropping his wooden cover, he moved quickly along the end of the building. Peering around the corner, he could see one of the large turtles down by the first barracks building.

He looked around him one more time to make sure there wasn't anyone nearby then sprinted for the opening in the security wall. It wasn't far and he covered the ground in about ten seconds.

Now that he was close to the opening he could see through to the turtle house and then the outer wall gate which was busted wide open. Happy that the path was open, he just kept on running and ran right out of the gate, turned right and ducked down behind the outer wall of the fort.

As Matt lay there catching his breath, he realized that this was almost the very spot where he and George Wu had scaled the wall to start this whole mess.

He jumped as he heard a burst of gun fire from behind him. He turned around scanning the grassy field. Then another burst of gunfire and he focused in on the sound, seeing someone lying on the ground about one hundred feet away. The soldier was prone and seemed to be shooting away from Matt, down the hill.

Murphy started crouch walking toward him. After he got a little closer he called out to the man, "Recon."

Rockford turned to look at him, and hastily motioned for Matt to join him, and he hurried the rest of the way.

"Good to see you Murphy," then looking around asked, "Where are the captain and the others?"

Matt just looked at him blankly, "I don't know. I was able to bust out on my own, well more or less. But they're going to be pinned down in there by the turtle, uh tank."

"The what?" Rockford asked.

Murphy quickly recounted to him what had happened over the previous day and a half. How he had discovered the tank disguised as a turtle, got captured, broke out and also what he saw as he fled the fort.

PFC Rockford listened but kept his gaze fixed down into the valley. "That is a whole lotta weird shit man," then his voice gained intensity, "Quick move!"

Matt obeyed, scrambling after Rockford until he came to a stop about 30 feet away. Back in their previous position Matt saw around a dozen arrows land in a circular group. *More arrows*, he thought.

The private smiled, "I've been keeping their asses pinned down, but every now and then they scoot up close for a volley. I usually reward their effort by dropping one of their archers. Then they go running back for cover. Mostly though, I'm just trying to keep their heads down until we can get the hell out of here."

Then he asked, "What about Wu?"

Matt pulled on the extra set of dog tags around his neck, "I never saw him after we were captured. The guys in there gave me these and indicated that he was dead. We both got hit on the head by a pipe or something, I think I was just lucky."

Rockford screwed up his face unhappily. Then he pulled his Beretta pistol and handed it to Matt, "Here, cover our backs. The plan was that once they found you guys, they'd come out this side of the fort and collect me. Else they'd pop a smoke grenade if they had to go out the other side."

Matt took the pistol and turned to look back in the direction of the fort. He didn't have to wait long before he saw a soldier come running out. His hope turned to disappointment when he saw it was only one man.

Private Cushman dropped down to a knee as he joined the other two men.

"Murphy! Great to see you're out," then in the next breath Cushman asked, "Where are captain and the others?"

Matt quickly told him about his capture and how he had escaped.

Cushman looked unhappy, "Crap, that means they're probably pinned down in there by that tank."

Cushman told the other two men how he had been able to knock the engine out on the other tank.

"I took a look at this one just now, but it's backed up against one of the buildings, I don't know if I can knock it out from the side. With that turtle skin I can't identify or aim at a weak spot."

Murphy thought for a moment then said, "If the captain and the others are inside, they'll know they're pinned. But if we can provide a way for them to get out, maybe they'll take it. How much smoke do you guys have?"

Rockford produced three smooth cased canister grenades.

Cushman said, "I got nothing. Had two for the 203 launcher but its back with Jenkins."

Murphy said, "I'm thinking we put all this smoke on that tank, and then hopefully Captain will see it and come out. What do you think?"

Cushman said, "Beats the hell out of my plan, cause I don't have one."

"How far can you throw one of these things Cush?" Murphy asked. Cushman was a big guy at 6 foot 1 and word had it he had played baseball in high school.

Cushman thought it over for a second and replied, "I think around 50 meters max."

"You're the guy then," said Murphy.

Cushman handed Murphy his rifle and took the three soup can sized grenades from Rockford.

Then Murphy said, "Rock, keep their heads down another minute or so, then once you see our smoke, fall back to cover the gate, and then... I don't know, hopefully captain will show and we can just get the hell out of here."

All three men nodded agreement and split up. Rockford let loose with another long burst of fire down into the military camp while Murphy and Cushman ran back to the fort.

Murphy, having the rifle, entered first through the broken gate, with Cushman close behind. Training the heavy rifle ahead of him, he took deliberate strides past the dragon house, then through the ruptured inner wall into the courtyard. So far he hadn't seen anyone.

Reaching the first building, one of the barracks, Private Murphy peeked around the corner and saw the turtle tank about 50 meters away, angled slightly away from him. This was the first time he got a good look at the faux snake that was coiled around the turret. *Weird.*

Around the tank were several warriors, some wearing their black armor, some not. There looked to be four armed with bows, the rest held pick axe type weapons.

Murphy turned the corner and knelt, bracing the rifle against the building, and aimed at the most exposed of the bowmen. Then Cushman came around behind him and hurled one of the steel canisters in a low trajectory toward the tank. Murphy watched it bounce several meters short of the target and come to rest precisely next to the big black monstrosity.

Almost immediately it burst and started spewing forth the brackish smoke. Heads turned in their direction as Cush lobbed another grenade. Murphy aimed and squeezed off a round at one of the archers, feeling the rifle's firm kick in his shoulder, but missed. He adjusted his aim and quickly fired again, downing the man who had just brought up his bow.

The second grenade was well short of the target, as intended, and was soon disgorging its contents as well. The tank was now almost completely obscured by smoke from the first grenade, but Murphy saw it rotate to face them.

Cushman ran back past Murphy giving a shout, "Let's go!"

Murphy turned and sprinted along behind Cushman until both were well outside the fort wall. They dropped down prone and watched the plume of smoke rising above the wall and waited in anticipation.

Chapter 37: Time to Go

Upon entering the large building, Captain Pearce, Sergeant Turner and PFC Bridgeman started by searching a number of small rooms but were met with disappointment. The rooms weren't locked and each housed one or two women, who had been shocked at their intrusion. Some were sleeping, some looked startled by all the noise outside, and one was even entertaining a male guest. They had checked around ten such rooms with no sign of Murphy or Wu.

Their assault on the base must have drawn all the warriors outside because they met no resistance at all inside the building. As they moved further into the large structure the space opened up. Then they came across a stairway leading to the second story.

The Captain said, "Let's come back to this, Bridgeman you stay here and guard the stairs. Turner, let's check out this door ahead."

There was a heavy door at the other end of the entry room. It was barred and Sergeant Turner pulled the pin up and out then gave the door a kick. It swung open to reveal a large dark room.

The captain heard a few gasps of surprise as he entered the room behind the sergeant and saw around 20 women huddled together on the far side of the windowless room. They looked on with fear and a few held their hands up shielding their eyes from the light spilling into the room.

Lt. Pontus' report on the first recon mission had speculated that they might run across something like this. It wasn't only men that had been taken captive from the surrounding countryside, but many young women and girls as well. It was a sure bet that these women had been mistreated since their abduction. As angry as it made Captain Pearce to think about, he didn't have the time or manpower to improve their situation at this time.

"Okay Sergeant, lets hit the stairs."

They left without a word, leaving the door open.

Then, all hell broke loose outside.

Captain Pearce heard the sound of wood splintering, then shortly afterwards the sound of sustained machinegun fire of a type he knew wasn't from anyone in his patrol. With the barrel of his rifle he pried the front door open a crack to see something unbelievable. A large brown and black object was moving past the building. It was draped with a segmented covering that had the appearance of a turtle shell. But from his angle he could clearly see tank tracks and the bottoms of four road wheel. Captain Pearce knew it was a light tank of some type and old because the engine sounded like a lawnmower.

Next he realized that it was probably engaging Private Camiroja. The captain had sworn and opened the door, firing into the side of it with his M4. It had no effect and the tank quickly moved out of sight behind a building in front of him.

"Sergeant, guard the door," he had said as he popped back inside, slamming the door shut. Then he tapped Private Bridgeman and approached the stairs. He wanted to find his missing soldiers and get out.

They charged up the stairs to find no one. The second story was mostly open space, with two doors on one wall and one on the opposite wall.

"Okay private, we're going to make a whirlwind check of these rooms. If you see anyone other than our guys, feel free to shoot."

The first two rooms held no one and nothing of note. But when they opened the third room, it revealed much. It too was devoid of people but the walls were covered with high quality maps of Korea. If the tanks hadn't already shown up to alter his reality, then these anachronisms would have done it.

"Bridgeman, grab a couple of those maps and let's get moving," he ordered.

Now, how to get past that tank.

As Pearce and Bridgeman went back down the stairs, he saw Sergeant Turner peering through a crack in the front door.

"Captain, a couple of smoke grenades are going off right out in front of the building. I'm pretty sure that I saw Murphy and Cushman deploy them," the sergeant said.

Well done men, the captain thought.

"Okay, then let's get the hell out of here while we can," the captain said. "You two head back toward the gate we came through, check on Camiroja. I'll cover you and be right on your tail."

Without further discussion the captain opened the front door and ran out to the corner of a medium sized building a short distance away while the other two men continued on to his left past the building.

Captain Pearce could hear the sound of the tank as it moved nearby. Through a break in the smoke he saw the side of it, perhaps 30 meters away and heading to his right. His M4 rifle had an M203 grenade launcher under the barrel inside of which was a single high explosive round. It wasn't designed to take out armored vehicles, but from the rear on a thin-skinned light tank it would probably do some harm.

He quickly adjusted his aim so it was appropriate for the launcher and fired the round, then ducked around the corner for cover from the blast. Instead of an explosion, all he heard was a loud metal on metal clang.

He peeked back around and though he couldn't see the tank he realized that because of the smoke he must have overestimated the distance to the target. Grenades fired from launchers had a safety mechanism that didn't arm the explosive until it had traveled 25 meters. His target must have been closer, and that was that. There was nothing else he could do, the tank would live to fight another day.

Not seeing any enemy personnel he started to run in the same direction that Turner and Bridgeman had gone. In just a few seconds he saw the open front gate and Bridgeman leveling his M4, firing a burst back into the fort. Beyond him, the captain caught a glimpse of Sergeant Turner dragging a soldier outside.

Bridgeman made eye contact with the captain and motioned for him to keep moving while he provided cover.

As he neared the gate, the captain saw two men lying on the ground bleeding. They weren't wearing the typical black armor of the enemy warriors. Instead they had on black uniforms, modern looking fitted clothing.

Exiting the fort Captain Pearce turned the corner and almost stopped in his tracks seeing another tank sitting right there, unmoving. He saw Sergeant Turner squatted down next to the tank and putting Private Camiroja over his shoulder. Then he moved off awkwardly toward the tree line.

The captain took a moment to scale the front of the fake turtle beast, poked the barrel of his M4 into the open top hatch and fired off a burst. Then he peered down into the tiny turret but didn't see anyone. He pulled back, took out a flash-bang grenade, pulled the pin, dropped it into the hatch, and then jumped down not waiting to see the effect.

He found himself running right next to Private Bridgeman toward the nearby woods, and then he heard the muffled boom of the grenade detonating. He didn't think it would destroy the tank, but it was all he could do with the weapons and time available.

They met up with the sergeant just beyond the first set of trees. He saw at once that Camiroja was dead, the front of his uniform was covered in blood.

As a group they made their way to where they had last seen Corporal Jenkins. He was watching them and keeping an eye on the area outside the fort. As they reached him he said, "Three of our guys just headed off west," he pointed away from the fort, "I think one of them was Murphy."

"Yeah, I saw him too," the Sergeant Turner said.

"That leaves Specialist Wu, hopefully Murphy will know where he is. Unfortunately, we're in no position to do anything about it, especially now with those tanks. We have no idea what we're dealing with. We've got to get to safety and link up with the other men."

The group gathered up their equipment and started moving west, further into the woods. Sergeant Turner carried Camiroja's lifeless body while Captain Pearce and Bridgeman helped Jenkins limp along.

Within 30 minutes, the group met up with Privates Cushman, Murphy and Rockford. They were all glad to be back together, but unsettled nonetheless.

Jenkins told the captain that he had sent Gan back to the village with a warning message. Captain Pearce commended the young NCO for his quick thinking.

As they collected themselves, Pearce thought about what had just happened. He was just as confused as to which way was up as when they had first come to this place after The Flash. But this time he had one dead soldier, and another MIA presumed dead as well.

Then he thought about the fort, and how deserted it felt. He wondered where everyone was. Then, a feeling of dread came over him.

Chapter 38: Onslaught

Lieutenant Chris Franks walked back to the observation post after checking out the backside of a tree, a typical morning ritual.

Four of his men were dutifully performing their assigned tasks. One of whom was scanning through the trees off into the distance with the spotting binoculars, another doing the same with a handheld pair. It was tough keeping focused when nothing happened hour after hour, day after day. For that reason Franks kept the duty rotating to a different man every hour.

It had been about a month since they had last seen anything interesting, unless you counted deer. He and his men had been rotating back and forth between manning the OP and working on things back at camp, Fort Somewhere. There was a second group of men that traded off with them for one week stretches being the eyes in the sky.

Lt. Franks and his men had just started their latest stint two days prior. During their most recent time back at camp, he had been impressed by just how much progress had been made on the housing project.

Franks walked up to Specialist Wilson, who had their smaller set of binoculars, and said, "Give your eyes a break Wilson, I'll take the duty for a while."

The young man looked up, smiled and handed the glasses over without hesitation, "Thank you sir."

The lieutenant sat and started scanning the area to the north of the village. All the nearby trees made it a really annoying task. You had to constantly ignore the distraction of big out of focus tree trunks running through your line of sight.

Franks wondered how his buddy Lieutenant Pontus was fairing on his campout.

He's probably sleeping in without a care in the world... jerk.

*   *   *

Lieutenant Pontus was running quickly through the brush, going up yet another ridgeline. Glancing back over his shoulder, he could see Meishan about 15 meters behind him. She was moving quickly, but couldn't quite keep up with his reckless pace.

John had considered leaving her at the camp thinking it might be safer there, but had quickly dismissed the idea. He didn't want her too far away from him.

He stopped and pulled out his small hand radio and switched it on, "Sky Mountain, come in Sky Mountain," he called into it, waiting for a reply.

Damn these mountains, he thought.

He checked his watch, they had been on the run for about an hour and he thought that they would be in radio range of the observation post by now. They had left all of their gear back at the campsite, only bringing water and John's radio and pistol.

Pontus hadn't seen any more airplanes, or anything else unusual, since that lone sighting. He was more and more convinced that the plane was of WWII vintage. But where had it come from?

Meishan arrived breathing heavily but in control, the sweaty green tank top clinging to her. She looked to him, not with anger or annoyance, but waiting to see what he would do or say next. It struck John how unselfish she was. She knew this wasn't about her and wasn't demanding his attention. "She's a keeper" he could recall his dad say of a woman with such qualities.

Pantomiming, he tried to say to her, "You stay here and rest. I'm going to go up on the ridge and try to call my men." John wasn't sure what words she heard, but she touched his chest and then pointed for him to go.

Go he did, running headlong through the forest once again. He was driven by the need to warn his men, to save lives. He didn't even know that it would matter if he warned them now or in three hours but he had to assume the worst.

As he ran, his mind churned over and over, *Where did it come from? Are there more? What else is out here?*

First they had come to this old world, by unknown means, and now a relic from the much more recent past had appeared. John felt like he was inside an old *Twilight Zone* episode.

In just a few minutes John would be at the crest of this ridge. Based on how long they had walked out, and how long he'd been running today, he thought for sure he would be able to contact the observation post once he was up there. He just hoped that his warning wouldn't come too late.

* * *

Specialist Reynolds was standing guard at the opposite end of the village from the road entrance. He was looking out across the river toward the machine gun emplacement watching "that female reporter" whose name he didn't know. She was just climbing up onto a small horse.

About 15 minutes earlier, he'd watched her arrive towing a small load of food and other supplies with some kind of sling contraption that dragged along on the ground behind the horse.

Heh, better check your lunch for horse shit boys, he thought with a crooked-toothed smile.

Now she was heading back to camp, bouncing along as the horse broke into a slow gallop.

Fine looking gal, he thought.

Nick Reynolds looked down at the quickly dwindling cigarette in his fingers and told himself, *last one until after lunch.*

Nick, and everyone else in the unit, had been in country for about two full months and just as food, fuel and other commodities had been dwindling all that time, so too had Nick's most treasured item, cigarettes.

He'd been quick to realize that cigarettes were going to be a highly sought after item and had started trading his water and food for them right away. He could deal with the suspect local water and bland food, just as long as he had his smokes.

"Hey Marl, uh, can I bum a smoke off of you?" his guard mate Private Kenny Harrison asked tentatively.

Nick looked back at him stone faced, took a long final drag off of his cig then flicked the butt away without a word.

A three pack a day man, Reynolds had almost immediately started rationing himself, trying to stretch his stock out. This had caused his already sour demeanor to turn downright surly. Now he was down to one carton, only *200* cigarettes, and limited himself to just a handful of smokes a day. Nick enjoyed smoking, and while he would readily admit to being addicted to them, he also considered himself to possess an iron will. He would stick to his self-imposed rationing, even if it did turn him into a complete ass.

Upon returning to camp after the last time he'd been on village guard detail he had made the mistake of popping off about hating the duty to his sergeant. Sarge wasn't one for taking crap from anyone let alone a member of his own squad. He had told Nick that now he'd have that duty "twenty-four-*seven*, three-sixty-*five!*"

Sargent Smith, who was also on guard detail this week, had had a few other choice words to say. Nick had grown up in a rough neighborhood but he hadn't heard some of the expressions that the grizzled sergeant had used. Yeah, sarge was a bit of an ass himself but Nick respected and responded to his kind of leadership, ass-*kicking*.

"Your mama told me not to let you smoke, junior. She said it might stunt your growth," Nick said stoically.

* * *

Lt. Franks usually started the observation chore in the seated position. Then as it became monotonous he'd stand and move around to get slightly different angles on what he was looking at, which usually helped him maintain vigilance.

It also helped when you saw something change, like now. Something caught the lieutenant's eye way out on the primitive road leading away from the village, at the point where it went out of view completely. They spent almost all of their time watching this very spot.

First two, three, then suddenly there were a dozen men walking down the road, all clad in black. *Here we go again*, Franks thought.

"Needham, get on the radio. Alert the village officer in charge that there could be an attack brewing. At least a dozen, and increasing, foot soldiers out on the road, one and a half kilometers away," he said quickly and calmly.

"Then alert Fort Somewhere of the situation so the colonel is informed," he continued.

"Yes sir."

Don't these guys learn? The lieutenant thought.

In the valley below he saw activity at Hornet's Nest, the fortified machinegun emplacement that had pretty much single handedly destroyed the enemy column in the previous attack. Franks watched the activity of the guards in the village, of which there were around ten at any one time aside from the machinegun nest. Then he switched back to scrutinizing the gathering force which had amassed to around 40 warriors.

That's strange, he thought because previously they had sent more than 100 men.

Lt. Franks continued to scan as far as he could see around the road, in the field below, along the river banks. He was sure there would be more.

In the valley below, an air horn sounded to spread the alert to everyone in the vicinity of the village that an attack was imminent.

Then Lt. Franks heard a gunshot, perhaps two, or maybe it was just an echo? It sounded like it was coming from somewhere close. He lowered the binoculars and looked at his men, who in turn were looking at him. Then they heard two more distinct shots, Franks was positive it was two this time.

Specialist Needham was listening intently on the radio, "Sir, the men at Hornet's Nest say they are taking gunfire from the east, they're yelling at us to cease fire."

The lieutenant curled his upper lip in surprise, "What? Tell them we aren't shooting at them, but we do confirm hearing gunshots." He started looking at the bottom of the slope they were on, but it was difficult to see much of anything but trees on the hill and tall grass in the valley below.

Who could be shooting? Chris thought. He recalled from one of the officer's briefings that there had been a couple of deserters from the unit. But they wouldn't be shooting at their own people, he hoped.

"Sir," came Specialist Needham's voice, "two men have been shot in the machinegun emplacement."

As the words were registering in Lt. Franks' mind, he suddenly saw approximately a dozen shapes rise up from the long grass down below at the foot of their hill. They were men, but elaborately camouflaged with grass and branches. They looked to be wielding bows.

The group came together in a clump for a moment and when they separated from their huddle they drew their bows as one man, and Franks caught a glimpse of... *fire*.

Shifting his gaze back to the machinegun nest, he saw arrows raining down on it, most of them on fire. Eight or ten of the arrows had struck the small log built enclosure, and it started to catch fire in multiple places.

"Needham, tell the guys in the M-G nest that they need to get out of there, it's starting to burn," his voice cracked slightly, "tell them to use the river for cover."

As the specialist relayed that information to the crew of the machinegun, Franks turned to the rest of his team.

"You two," he pointed, "move down slope and find a place you can put some rifle fire on those archers, but stay as concealed as you can. Someone in their group has a gun…"

*   *   *

Specialist Reynolds was in the middle of a debate. Though he had told himself that he wouldn't have another smoke until after lunch, his mood was particularly bad this morning and he was craving another.

Then he heard the air horn, signaling trouble. That sealed the deal and he jumped down into his foxhole to retrieve another smoke out of his pack.

Next Nick heard distant gun shots ring out as he was sitting on the edge of his foxhole, just lighting up. Private Harrison was walking towards him a short distance away.

"I can't believe these guys are attacking again, I mean they're using bows and arrows! I feel sorry for them," Harrison said.

Nick shook his head at the naïve teenager's words as he leaned down to drop his lighter back into his pack.

Then he heard a whooshing sound, and another and another, right near his head. In the ground nearby a short stick was suddenly pointing up out of the ground. Nick fell awkwardly into his fox hole, then righted himself and peered out.

He saw Harrison clutching his neck, something black was sticking out through the front of it, and blood was quickly seeping out from between his fingers. His face held shock and confusion. He stood a second longer then fell to his knees, then onto his face. Then Reynolds saw that there were three arrows sticking out of the young man's back besides the one in his neck.

He felt sorry for the kid, and momentarily guilty for not being nicer to him, then he felt something hit the front of his Kevlar helmet, and more whooshing sounds as several more of the small black shafted arrows swirled around his head and he ducked down once again.

Sticking out of the wall of his foxhole was the fletching of an arrow. He pulled it out of the dirt, and saw that it was short like a crossbow bolt. The tip was metal and had two sharp edges, but the tip was fairly blunt.

Readying his M4 rifle, Nick popped up just enough to see out of the hole and fired off a long burst into the nearby woods, where he assumed the attackers were. He couldn't see anyone, but hoped that would discourage them for a moment.

Reynolds then reached over and grabbed the wood cover to his fox hole and pulled it over himself. He left just a small crack so he could peek out toward the unseen enemy.

Then he heard sporadic gunfire from within the village itself.

Sticking the muzzle of his rifle out into the small sliver of light coming into his hole, he watched and didn't have to wait long. Several men came out of the forest, all wearing black armor. Some held crossbows at the ready, others small swords. They split up, some moving into the village and he couldn't see them after they went behind a hut. The others were walking quickly toward him, six in all about 25 meters away with weapons at the ready.

Nick decided it was time to pick a contestant. He aimed at one of the bowmen and fired a single shot. The man's head jerked back and he fell. The others dropped down out of sight.

A winner! he thought.

Reynolds pulled a grenade off of his belt and prepared to toss it out. He slid the cover of his foxhole back about a foot, pulled the pin and chucked it in the direction of his attackers. Unfortunately he didn't have any lethal grenades, just a tear gas grenade. He pulled the cover closed over his hole and waited.

Sitting duck, he thought then, *no, fish in a barrel.*

Nick thought about making a run for cover, but which direction?

More gunfire, this time closer, sporadic individual shots, not machinegun fire. Then he heard cries of pain, multiple people were hurt, all around him.

> Specialist Reynolds didn't scare easily but being in the dark hole surrounded by the noise of battle and screams made his blood run cold.
>
> He sucked hard on his cigarette and hoped it wouldn't be his last.

* * *

Private Greg Vaughn was standing behind the clinic, near the river when the call had come down from the OP that enemy combatants were approaching the village. He and his fellow guard, PFC Nancy Joiner, were roving guards and moved throughout the village during their post.

They were loosely assigned to be with the officer in charge, in this case Lt. Norman, who also roamed during the watch. The lieutenant held a portable radio and Vaughn had heard the call come in. Then they heard gunfire and saw the flaming arrows. It was more than two hundred meters away, but they could clearly see the machinegun emplacement was burning.

At first their trio had taken cover behind the clinic. But then they had seen movement in the thinly forested slope just west of the village. This was at their backs, so they went back to their original location and took cover from this closer, more imminent threat.

Greg had keen eyes and wanted to engage the shapes he could make out in the trees, but it was possible that they were merely villagers gathering wood or food, so he had to be disciplined and wait.

Then he saw six or eight men move down into the village, some with crossbows and some with double edged swords. He yelled to the lieutenant, "I have several armed men moving into the village. Permission to fire?"

"Granted!" the lieutenant shouted.

Vaughn aimed and fired at first one target, then another, then another. Hitting them all with relative ease. A typical M4 rifle had very little recoil as is, but his had an M203 grenade launcher attached under the barrel which added weight and reduced muzzle climb to nil.

"Joiner," he called to his partner, "head over to that hut, I'll cover you."

The young woman readied her rifle and did as he instructed, covering the ten meters quickly and putting her back to the small hut.

Lieutenant Norman just stood behind him, not saying much of anything. Vaughn had recognized Norman as a liability early in his few months serving under him and didn't intend to wait for his instructions.

Vaughn could see more men spreading out into the village from the hillside. At least a dozen, perhaps more. He wanted to try and contain them somehow.

There were two more soldiers a short distance to his right, so he thought it best for he and Joiner to shore up the left side. He ran and joined Private Joiner and the two of them leapfrogged down a few more huts and then started watching for targets to come their way. Greg was intent on holding the ground on the south side of the village.

* * *

Back at the OP, Lt. Franks was watching the whole mess unfold in the valley before him like a wargame exercise. Several of the guards in the village appeared to be pinned down and enemy soldiers were running rampant in the village. He feared the soldiers in the village might get overrun.

Franks' men Wilson and Hogan had moved down close to the valley and were shooting at the archers that had set the machinegun emplacement on fire. He had seen them score a few hits and it looked like they were keeping the archers pinned. There also hadn't been any more enemy gunfire that he could tell.

Franks looked off into the distance, back down the road, to check on enemy activity. What he saw was perplexing. Two large objects moving on the road, *wagons*? They were a mottled black and brown color. He didn't see horses pulling them, *are they being pushed*? he wondered.

The two objects were moving in tandem along the road, then the one in the rear made a quick pivot about 60 degrees to its left moving off-road onto the grass. Lt. Franks had seen that telltale pivot turn many times in his stint in the Army, it was always associated with tracked vehicles.

Franks put down the general purpose binoculars he'd been using to monitor the fighting and moved over to the much more powerful tripod mounted spotting glasses. Training them on the black vehicle moving across the grassy field he saw that it had the general shape of a tank.

Oddly, it was camouflaged up to look like an animal, a turtle, with something sitting on its back, a coiled serpent perhaps. He wasn't sure if it was supposed to be two separate things or one combined creature like a chimera. In either case, Franks' assessment was that it didn't quite pull off the trick.

Turtles just aren't that big, he thought.

From the head of the snake like coil, he saw a flash and a puff of smoke. Franks raised his head up from the binoculars just in time to see an explosion tear a hole in the machinegun bunker. Followed by the sounds of the cannon bark and the boom of the explosion below.

"What the hell was that?" asked Specialist Needham.

"It's cannon fire! There are two tanks down there, most definitely not ours," the lieutenant yelled. "Warn everyone that there are two camouflaged light tanks moving toward the village. Then get Fort Somewhere on the line."

Lt. Franks' mind raced trying to figure out what he was seeing, what was happening. Besides the soldiers getting routed, now he feared that the whole village might get flattened and all the villagers killed.

"I have the colonel sir," Needham said.

Franks grabbed the radio and blurted out, "Colonel, this is Lieutenant Franks. There are two tanks, I say again two armored vehicles attacking the village."

Through the voice on the line, Franks could hear the disbelief, "What…? ours?"

"No sir, they're not Abrams or Bradley types, they're smaller. Light tanks, armed with a small caliber cannon," Lieutenant Franks replied. "Colonel, we need help, I don't think we have any anti-tank weapons in the village and our only medium machinegun is knocked out."

"I'll get you some as fast as I can, but you know it'll take at least twenty minutes…" the colonel's reply hung in the air as he didn't have to add, *but that will be too late.*

"I understand sir, I'll keep you informed," the lieutenant replied soberly and gave the handset back to Needham.

Franks returned to watching the battle, powerless to help.

Chapter 39: Dagger-Axe vs. Claymore

Specialist Dominic Jones sat in his foxhole near the main entrance to the village thinking, *Maybe things weren't so boring back at camp.*

It had been a month since Jones had been hit in the shoulder by an arrow during the first enemy assault on the village. During that time he'd mostly been sitting on his butt in Fort Somewhere, left arm pretty much useless. Fortunately he was right handed.

He hadn't been much help on construction in Fort Somewhere beyond offering some advice, he was pretty handy back home. He'd also carried some of the lighter supplies, one handed, up and down the hill, to alleviate boredom more than anything.

The doctor had allowed him to start using his arm the previous week, it was stiff and sore as hell but he used it as much as possible. He'd lobbied Sergeant Smith to let him come back onto the village patrol rotation, demonstrating that he could hold his rifle properly.

So here he was, hiding in a hole, taking pot shots out of it occasionally to try and keep the enemy away. And he'd *begged* to be here.

A few feet away Sergeant Smith was leaning up over the edge of his hole firing at whatever presented itself. They were taking turns suppressing the enemy that had infiltrated the village. Jones popped up and looked over at the sergeant. There was a small arrow sticking through the side of his helmet. It hadn't penetrated the hard shell but rather looked to be caught underneath the camouflaged fabric helmet cover. It hadn't caused any injury to the sergeant, but it looked hilarious.

Jones was splitting his time looking into the village and behind them on the road, the initial warning said that foot soldiers were approaching. He was looking back that way when he heard the loud report of a cannon.

He tried to locate the source of the sound and then spotted a vehicle moving through the field about four hundred meters away. It was camouflaged but looked like it might be a small tank or halftrack.

"Sarge, check this shit out," Jones called.

As they were both studying the mystery vehicle, a call came on the radio.

"Be advised there appear to be two small tanks approaching the village from the north. One in the field, one on the road," the voice said.

Jones said, "Sarge, we got anything for that?"

Smith wrinkled up his nose, "I don't think we can touch that one out there, but if the other one stays on the road and comes in close, I got something for *that* mother." The sergeant reached down inside the foxhole and checked a control box, "You keep your eyes on the village and watch my back."

Jones nodded and gave a slight smile.

Dominic pulled the cover for his foxhole closer, sliding it around to the village side. Then he propped it up at an angle using his backpack and leaned his rifle over it. This would not only give him pretty good cover from incoming arrows, it eased the throbbing in his shoulder as he could just steady the rifle with one hand until he had something to shoot at.

Within the village, Dominic could hear occasional gunfire. Also, the sounds of injured people yelling, and villagers screaming in fear. He felt compelled to get in there and help, but he and the sergeant had to hold their position next to the road and try to stop anyone and anything that approached.

Within another couple of minutes he heard the sergeant say, "Here it comes."

Jones peeked around behind him and about two hundred meters away was the tank, rolling along slow and steady, with at least two dozen warriors walking beside and behind it.

"Head down and keep it down," the sergeant commanded. Jones didn't hesitate.

After another 30 seconds, Jones took a quick peek down the road and saw that the tank, definitely a tank, was just 100 meters away, right where a mound of dirt next to the road started and led almost all the way to Jones' position.

They had built that mound over a month earlier in preparation for a possible attack on the village. The attack came, but the deadly secret hidden within the berm hadn't been needed that day. In the time since, grass had started growing all along the length of the dirt mound, and even some wild flowers.

"Ready..." the sergeant warned, "Get ready... firing... now!"

Within the berm were a series of Claymore mines. Unlike your typical land mine, these weren't meant to be stepped on, and rather than blowing up out of the ground, each one fired several hundred tiny steel balls out across the ground. Each one was like 40 shotguns going off all at once.

Three of the devices spread out over 50 meters, pointing across the road, detonated at one time. The bizarre looking turtle tank was right next to the middle of the set, and the force of the explosion rocked the metal monster and quickly obscured it in a cloud of dirt.

A few seconds later, the disheveled beast emerged out the dust, its turtle shell shredded and mostly missing on one side, its small angular hull showing itself. Then it ran over the dirt berm and lodged itself awkwardly into the base of the slope.

Behind the tank the score or more of warriors walking in its wake had been hit by the little ball bearings from the last Claymore in the line to devastating effect. Jones was glad that he couldn't see them very well through the dust, but he did hear them.

* * *

Private Greg Vaughn heard the detonation of the Claymore mines clearly from his position, barely a hundred meters away.

He looked around the corner of the clinic and was very satisfied to see that one of the tanks looked to be incapacitated.

Opposition in the village had lightened some. He and PFC Nancy Joiner had taken care of four swordsmen that had attempted to flank them and were considering doing a sweep through the village when the tanks had appeared.

Now that one was knocked out, Vaughn looked to the other, sitting several hundred meters away. Then it started to move, angling toward the village entrance where the other tank was sitting disabled.

Vaughn's pulse quickened as he came up with an idea. While the tank had been sitting far away in an empty field there hadn't been anything he could do. But now that it was coming closer, he could approach it behind some cover.

He ducked down and ran past the clinic, livestock pen and a small field of millet then laid down on the backside of a slight hill.

He crawled to the crest and saw the tank was continuing to close on the village then he saw and heard it fire its canon toward the village entrance, where he knew two soldiers were. The tank was still about two hundred meters away from him, but its path of approach should bring it to within one hundred or less, and show him its side.

Beautiful.

Ducking back down, Vaughn opened the breech of the M203 grenade launcher attached to the barrel of his rifle. He removed the high explosive shell and replaced it with the more lethal high explosive dual purpose one which could penetrate lightly armored vehicles. He just hoped this tank was *light* enough.

Vaughn was pretty sure that a direct hit from the side or back would immobilize the tank. But he didn't want to chance his only shot on a frontal attack, where tanks had their thickest armor, so he waited.

Then he heard the sound of machinegun fire from just over the hill. He crawled cautiously up the slope and saw the tank had come to a stop and was firing a machinegun into the village. It was almost close enough for him to try a shot.

Looking to his left he saw little puffs of dirt indicating where the bullets were impacting. It was right near the foxholes at the village entrance, and he also saw evidence that some of the huts in the village where taking hits as well.

Can't wait, he thought.

Rolling off to his right, Private Vaughn jumped to his feet and sprinted 20 meters to get a straight on shot on the side of the target. Then he stopped, dropped to a knee, aimed his weapon right in the middle of the strangely decorated vehicle, and fired.

Vaughn watched as the relatively slow grenade took a full second to reach the tank, the longest second of his life. Then he saw a small explosion split the thin turtle shell open from underneath. A split second later a large internal explosion burst the tank at the seams.

Touchdown.

* * *

As the noise of battle was subsiding Specialist Reynolds sat in his fox hole, M4 carbine clutched against his chest, cigarette hanging from his mouth. He was surprised to still be alive.

It seemed an eternity that he'd been crouched in this hole, but based on the two cigarettes he'd smoked, and the third in his mouth, he was thinking.

Ten minutes? Fifteen?

He heard the sound of footsteps approaching and got ready to put a bullet into anyone that came calling.

Then he heard a voice say, "Hey Marl, you okay?"

Then Nick saw a hand reach under the lid to his spider hole and slide it off. The bright sky dazzled him, then he saw the familiar face of PFC Carson.

Carson knelt down and said with concern, "Are you hit Nick?"

Nick came to his senses and slowly started to stand up straight, shaking his head, "No... I think I'm fine."

To his left he saw Private Pulaski looking at the body of Private Harrison.

With an arm hold from Carson, Nick climbed out of his hole. He looked around and saw that there were five, no, six black clad bodies lying within ten meters.

Carson said, "You made great bait man. These guys kept trying to get in close and get you and we just kept droppin 'em."

Private Pulaski joined them and said, "He's gone, multiple arrow strikes in his back, he must have died quickly," he paused briefly. "I can't believe they killed Kenny."

"Alright, let's go link up with the L-T and Sergeant Smith," Carson said.

Nick joined the other two as they moved through the village keeping an eye out for enemy personnel. Along the way they found a few injured villagers and some dead.

As they reached the middle of the village Nick saw the door to a hut just ahead of them swing open and one of the warriors strode out fixing his gaze on him. After a moment of indecision the man raised his bloodied sword. This ended up being his final act on Earth as Carson put a bullet in him.

The trio soon met up with the rest of the village guard detail, Lieutenant Norman, Sergeant Smith and three others, all of whom were well. Together they shared the euphoria of having survived a trial of life and death. The battle was over.

Nick listened as Dominic Jones praised Private Vaughn for taking out the second tank, the one that had him pinned down in his fox hole and "scared outta my mind."

As the smoke settled Dr. Stone and two medics worked their way through the carnage in and around the village. In all there were two dead soldiers and one badly wounded. Additionally four villagers had been seriously wounded and five were dead. Hearing the tally the men, and woman, who had bravely fought off the attack realized soberly that even in victory there were losses.

Chapter 40: Grieves

Lang knelt on the floor of his family's hut, trying to block out the wailing of his sister, Jin, who was kneeling just next to him. He needed to savor his own grief. Before him, wrapped in cloth, was the lifeless body of his other sister, Yin.

His mother was praying and hoping that Yin's spirit would return, but Lang had seen what the sword had done to his sister. Her body was not a suitable vessel to house her spirit any longer. His sister was gone.

Lang was assessing shares of blame for his beloved sister's death. The first share went to himself. He had been away from the village at the time of the attack, hunting in the woods to the west. If he had been at home, he could have cut down the vile creature that killed Yin, or at least taken the sword meant for her.

He could have used his stolen thunder bow to destroy the brute that had attacked the small defenseless girl. But he had yet to learn how it worked, in fact had been afraid to touch it, so it remained buried.

That ends today.

Someone was at the door, it was Meishan. She entered quickly, and then fell to the floor and cried. Lang remained stoic, looking down at his sister.

He could hear Jin and Meishan crying and saw out of the corner of his eye that they were embracing.

Lang had not, would not embrace his sister, or his mother. He would not allow himself to be consoled. No one knew how he felt. Though each of them had grief of their own, his grief was *his* and he had recoiled from their touch.

Then he sensed a calming presence and felt her hand on his shoulder.

"Lang, I am sorry she is gone, she was a wonderful sister and friend," came Meishan's sobbing voice.

His wall could not withstand her attack. He turned and she embraced him tightly. Though he was larger than she, Lang was a few years younger and he felt a little like a child in her arms. He started to cry.

He felt the healing power of her body as it pressed against him and allowed his twofold grief to come out; grief at the loss of a sister, grief at the loss of this woman who held him, both women that he loved.

Meishan loosened her hold on him and looked into his eyes.

"Brother, I will be here for you and your family in this time of sorrow," and then she let him go. She turned and found his mother and put her arms around her.

The word "brother" though spoken with compassion, made his heart shudder and darkness encircled his mind once again.

The second person requiring blame for Yin's death was the vermin who had run her through. But one of the green men had already killed him. Though Lang was glad he was suffering eternal punishment, and that the rest of his family was safe, it denied him the chance to sink his sword into the man whose hands were responsible. But others could be made to pay.

Lastly, these green men who had come in uninvited, they held the final share of blame. They had angered the enemy and caused this attack. It had been unnecessary.

Lang suppressed any and all reasons that might absolve them from part of the blame for his sister's death. Even the fact that his very life was owed to them was suppressed.

The green men can pay their share, and I have the tool to make this happen, he thought and he plotted. And the one that would be made to pay was a simple choice. *He* had caused the loss of two pieces of Lang's heart. John would pay for that with his life.

For now though he returned his focus to sister. She deserved what was left of his heart in this time of mourning. The time for vengeance would come later.

Chapter 41: We Are Not Alone

The day after the battle to defend the village Colonel Erickson sat in the village meeting hall with Major Baker and most of his senior officers. Also present were Lt. Pontus and some of the men who had been directly involved in the battle for the village.

The colonel was reviewing the current status for everyone so they were all in sync. "Captain Pearce's patrol radioed in last night. As the note we got from the runner they sent indicated, they met with tanks at the fort. There is one KIA and one MIA, presumed dead. They also have one man with a leg injury so they will be slow in coming back."

"Obviously the presence of tanks, and other modern equipment throws some confusion into our theory of time travel, but we still don't know how to explain the lack of other signs of an advanced civilization. Let's go over what we know one thing at a time," the colonel said.

"First, the tanks. Captain?" the colonel looked at Captain James commander of the tanks of H Company, and an expert on armored fighting vehicles.

"Yes sir. I went all through the vehicle, and there is no doubt its design is that of a World War Two Japanese tank, most closely resembling the Type 95 light tank. It has a 37 millimeter cannon and both bow and turret mounted seven point seven millimeter machine guns," the captain said.

"Markings inside all appear to be in Japanese, but I'm going to see if we have someone in the unit that can read Japanese to confirm," he continued. "It's in good operating condition so hard to tell how old it is. The North Koreans may have operated similar tanks back in the First Korean War, but why they would still have them is beyond me."

"Aside from the thrown track and a few holes it's functional. It has a full load of ammo and an almost full tank of diesel fuel," James concluded.

"How about the destroyed tank?" Major Baker asked.

"Looks like it's the same type, road wheels and tracks are the same. Size is the same, but it's a total loss. Onboard ammo and fuel burned the hull out," the captain replied.

"Okay, Lieutenant Pontus tell us what you encountered," the colonel said.

The lieutenant cleared his throat and began, "I was just a few klicks south east of the village and had an airplane fly almost right over me." He described the design of the aircraft and its odd dragon paint scheme.

"I sketched out what I saw best I could and went over it with Doctor Stone since he's a private pilot and airplane enthusiast," John said motioning to the doctor seated next to him.

Dr. Stone spoke, "Based on his sketch and description, it appears to have been a Japanese Val dive-bomber, or similar model. This type of aircraft was used by the Japanese in the attack on Pearl Harbor at the start of World War Two, and throughout the war," the lieutenant said.

"So what's with all this trickery? Tanks dressed up like turtles, airplanes like dragons?" Major Baker wanted to know.

"Let's come back to that Major," Erickson redirected. "Sergeant Paulson, show us what you have."

The sergeant produced a brass casing from his shirt pocket and placed it on the small table they were gathered around.

"I was in the machinegun nest when we heard the first set of shots. Private Donaldson was hit bad, he didn't have much of a chance. Then two seconds later, Martinez was hit too, but not as badly," the sergeant fought with his emotions as he spoke.

"As the flaming arrows came in I got both of them out and down into the river for cover. Donaldson died right there in the water…" the sergeant said.

"Once the reinforcements arrived to secure the village, I handed my guys off to a medic. Then went to look for the snipers that got them," he said with fierceness in his eyes. "I didn't find them, but I found where they'd been laying, confirmed by this spent case."

The sergeant regained his composure and continued, "There isn't a head stamp on the casing and it doesn't match any ammo we have. But I could tell it was roughly thirty caliber like what our EBR and M240 machinegun fires."

Paulson turned and gestured to Captain James. "After looking at the guns the captain recovered from that tank, the ammo is a match. Japanese seven point seven millimeter."

Colonel Erickson was proud of Sergeant Paulson's actions and bravery. He wished that it didn't take dire circumstances for such characteristics to be put on display.

The colonel looked around at his men and voiced what he thought they were thinking, "So where did all this hardware come from? Why all these Second World War relics here?"

Dr. Stone made an odd face that caught the colonel's eye.

"Major Stone? Something wrong?" Erickson asked.

"No Colonel, it's just that, well… Isn't it obvious?" he said with a slightly condescending tone.

All the eyes around the table were on him.

Damon Stone shifted to a more serious demeanor as he began, "What I mean to say is that, I think we should expect to find a very large Japanese influence in the region, especially if we were to head further south along the Korean peninsula, and thus closer to the Japanese Home Islands."

"But where did they come from and how did they get here?" Major Baker asked.

"The same way we did of course... as the unintended byproduct of a nuclear bomb detonation," Damon Stone answered plainly.

There it was, that thing that the colonel had been staring at since this whole series of events unfolded. Somehow it actually made sense, made everything else click into place.

"The flash..." Erickson said with reflection.

"You think that we got hit by a nuke, and that's how we got here?" Major Baker said incredulously.

"Well, in a manner of speaking yes. But a better way to look at it might be to say that, a nuclear weapon detonation created a facsimile of us in this parallel universe," he paused a moment. "I'm sorry to say it but, I'd wager that back in our previous time we're dead in the middle of a big crater, along with most of the regiment."

The faces in the room were stark, sullen.

The colonel broke the silence, "And the Japanese, the same thing happened to them when we dropped the a-bombs on them back in nineteen forty-five? So, how long have they been here in the past?" the colonel asked.

The doctor's face took on an analytical expression, "Well let's assume for a moment that this incredible side effect of an atomic weapon is fairly consistent in its effect. That would mean that for roughly 70 years the relatively modern cities of Hiroshima and Nagasaki have had free reign over ancient Japan, Korea and anywhere else that they have cared to venture forth into."

"If that's true," said Major Baker, clearly struggling, "why are they using such old weapons? Certainly they could have created much more advanced tanks and weapons in 70 years?"

"Necessity is the mother of invention Major," the colonel said, while Dr. Stone nodded in agreement. "Rapid advances in weaponry typically happen during a war or the threat of war. You have to because the other side is always building a bigger stick, if you don't keep up you lose."

Dr. Stone added, "Against these Bronze Age people, the weaponry the Japanese possessed in 1945 are just as far beyond them as anything we have. The basic unit of land warfare hasn't changed, it's essentially still a man with a rifle."

"It's only now, against our 21st Century weapons, that what the Japanese have would prove inadequate," Stone stated. "Though, as we've seen, an old rifle or an arrow can still kill a man no matter what time he's from," he said solemnly.

Their discussion was interrupted by commotion from outside. As a group they stood, Colonel Erickson reaching the door of the first.

As he got outside, several soldiers were yelling to each other. One saw the colonel and said, "Sir, aircraft above!" pointing to the north.

The colonel heard the noise now, the buzzing of more than one engine blending into a droning sound. Backing up away from the nearby tree covered hills, he finally spotted two aircraft moving in an arc around the north side of the village at low altitude.

"Everyone take cover and do NOT fire your weapons!" the colonel ordered. There was now a full platoon stationed in the village and heavily armed. But they didn't have anything that would be effective against aircraft ready as yet and he didn't want to give them a reason to strafe the village with machineguns.

Then Erickson watched in horror as the first of the two planes dipped its left wing toward the village, banking and coming at them in a shallow dive. This aircraft had the same dragon paint scheme that Lt. Pontus had described. As it approached, smoke started billowing from the side of the nose, just aft of the engine, leaving a long grey trail.

It was boring in on something and then the colonel saw twin rapid flashes from the nose of the plane, machinegun fire. It wasn't aiming at the village however. Erickson followed the plane's path with his eyes and saw a stationary Humvee that was quickly pock marked with holes and its glass splintered.

The aircraft pulled up and made a graceful climbing loop, joining its wingman, and both planes flew on west. The colonel noticed that there were small objects, bombs, under the wings of both planes.

Erickson watched for a moment and then realized...

He ran to where a radio was kept outside the clinic and grabbed the handset.

"Sky Mountain this is Colonel Erickson in the village," he said intensely.

"This is Sky Mountain, go ahead Colonel," the voice replied.

"Get a hold of Colonel Brower at Fort Somewhere. Tell him an air attack is imminent. I say again, an air attack on his position is *imminent*. Two light bombers inbound!"

So far they had been fortunate, casualties to his unit had been light. But the enemy had the initiative and seemed intent on taking advantage of that fact.

Colonel Erickson realized now that he had underestimated the enemy. In assuming they only had bows and arrows he had shown mercy that had likely cost lives. Lives of his men, and lives of men and women in the village. A primitive enemy did not mean a stupid one. In fact, whoever planned the most recent attack on the village had shown great skill.

He decided then and there that it was time to learn from his mistakes and gain control of the situation.

Chapter 42: Air Raid

Lieutenant Franks sat atop one of his teams' Bradleys up on the hill of Fort Somewhere. The camouflage netting that had been covering the armored vehicle was pulled most of the way back, giving him an unobstructed view. Not really much of a fort he thought, there's no wall, no defenses of any kind really, except the men and vehicles.

The day before, the battle in the village, had been intense. Sitting in the observation post watching the carnage but being unable to help had left Franks rattled and unnerved. Fortunately when the smoke had settled, it hadn't been as bad as he'd feared it would be at the height of the engagement.

After the battle, fresh troops had been put on village guard detail and the second crew brought in to staff the OP, relieving Franks and his men who had all headed back to the main camp.

After a fitful night of not sleeping, Chris Franks had been glad to see the sun. It brought a newness that helped to wash away the memories of the previous day.

He was running a check on the systems in one of his two M6 Linebackers, to make sure it would be ready if needed. It had been sitting mostly idle for the past two months. Ironically, his two M6s might actually come in handy after all. The night before, his friend John Pontus had told him that he'd actually seen an *airplane*.

Lt. Franks called down into the hull of the modified Bradley, "So is the battery dead or can we turn it over?"

A dull voice came back to him up through the open turret hatch, "I don't know. Last time we ran it, it started fine and we ran it long so it should have charged the battery. Now it's almost dead again, I think that battery is bad."

Franks sighed, "Okay, I think there are some spares." Then he smiled to himself, "If not, we can pull a battery out of one of the less mission-critical vehicles."

Then the noise of an ambulance siren broke the peaceful morning calm. This was a prearranged warning signal for the camp.

Franks looked around. He could see down into the valley where most of the units' men and vehicles were stationed, and saw that some men were running.

Dropping down into the turret, he switched the radio on to contact the primary command vehicle, the only vehicle in camp that was allowed to run a generator. It maintained radio contact with the OP in the village.

"Camp Nowhere, this is Lieutenant Franks, what's going on?"

The voice of Lieutenant Colonel Brower came back to him, "Lieutenant we've been warned that an air attack on our position is imminent. Two fixed wing aircraft. What is the status of our air defenses?"

Air defenses? Lt. Franks thought. Just last week his vehicles had been gathering moss, now they wanted air defenses.

"Sir, I'm sitting in one of our two M6s right now, but we really aren't ready for anything," the lieutenant said.

"Well then you might want to *get* ready," the voice boomed.

"Wilson, try and get this thing started!" Franks yelled to his crewman while scrambling up to look out the turret. He heard the diesel trying to start, but it just chattered on without firing up.

His head outside the turret once again, Lieutenant Franks scanned the sky and listened for the sound of aircraft.

He called back down to Specialist Wilson, "Forget it, save what's left of the battery. Maybe we can get the camo net off of the other one before…"

Then he saw an object move in over the top of the mountain on the opposite side of the valley. It was a fixed wing, propeller driven airplane in a steep dive heading into the valley.

Muttering a curse to himself, Franks grabbed the turret slew control and he felt the turret swivel quickly to the right, as he brought it to bear on the attacking aircraft.

"Wilson, target, airplane, get ready to fire Stinger missile," he ordered.

Lieutenant Franks watched the plane getting closer, it was coming in fast and he wouldn't be able to shoot at it before it could hit a target. Then he saw two small objects fall from the outer wings of the dive bomber and then it pulled up steeply and banked away.

The two bombs created a thunderous explosion as they hit near a parked vehicle partially obscured by camo netting. Franks wasn't sure if it was a tank, truck or Bradley.

"Ready," came Wilson's voice. Franks just shook his head in anger at once again being helpless to stop an attack.

Then a second aircraft, this one coming down the valley from the northeast in a fairly level flight path. Franks knew it was on a strafing run, its guns were probably only seconds from cutting loose.

Turning the turret back to the left slightly, he called out, "target, airplane."

"I have the target, and...and a strong tone from the missile," Wilson replied.

"Fire!"

From the long metal box sticking up above the turret next to Franks, one of the four small Stinger missiles contained within popped out of its casing, leaping forward 50 feet. A split second later its rocket motor ignited, rapidly accelerating it to over 1,000 miles per hour. The Val dive bomber was flying at about 200 hundred mph on a straight and level path. Homing in on the heat of the target plane's engine, the little missile was still accelerating when it impacted just aft of the engine cowling.

A millisecond later it exploded, blowing the cowling off of the airplane entirely. Jagged pieces of the plane's skin floated like chaff in the air. The engine was wrecked and the plane lost all thrust in that moment.

Franks watched with excitement as the bomber pitched up slightly and started a slow roll banking away from him. A few seconds later it impacted one of the foothills rising up from the valley and disappeared into the trees. Another second and it revealed itself again as a bright orange fireball.

"Good kill Wilson, good job," Lieutenant Franks called down to the enlisted man. "Get ready for number two."

Franks scanned for the second airplane. He didn't have to wait long.

Just to the right of the rising smoke column from the first destroyed aircraft, he saw the second appear, and it was moving headlong toward him.

Again grabbing the turret control, Franks jammed it right to bring the missiles around to bear on the incoming target and... nothing happened. Simultaneously Wilson called up.

"I got nothing down here, battery is dead sir."

Franks started to crank the turret manually, but in his gut he realized he'd never bring it around in time to meet the threat. Just as his mind was figuring this out as well, twin flashes erupted from the nose of the small bomber.

Lt. Franks had just enough time and presence of mind to slam his hatch shut before hearing the first of several dozen bullets striking the armored hull and turret of his Bradley. He hoped the enemy aircraft's guns were something relatively small like .30 caliber, which the armor *should* protect them from.

Then the bullets stopped and he heard the plane fly over, then Franks got into motion.

229

Dropping down through the turret and into the rear hull where the scouts sit, Franks slid one of the extra Stinger missile tubes from storage. Wilson was right behind him and picked up a grip stock unit and, one after the other, they existed through the open troop hatch. Once out they combined their two items together and activated the system.

Franks raised the cumbersome 35 pound Stinger launcher and searched the skies, looking for trouble. He watched and waited, but their attacker didn't return.

Franks spoke with Colonel Brower. Amazingly, no one was hurt during the brief air attack. The small bombs dropped by the first plane struck near one of the not well hidden M1 tanks. The near miss hadn't been nearly enough to disturb the heavily armored Abrams tank, and no personnel had been in the area.

After that, Lt. Franks got his crews on alert and both M6 Linebackers operational, after acquiring a replacement battery. One remained up on the hill and the other moved out into the valley, to give wider coverage and a better line of sight up the valley.

They also setup a Sentinel portable radar system. It was placed high on the hill of Fort Somewhere where it started sweeping the skies with electromagnetic energy, looking for other aircraft. Early warning was essential for air defense and next time, the enemy might decide to send more than two lightly armed scout birds.

If they came, Franks knew his teams would be ready. Besides the two Linebackers which could quickly fire up to 4 Stingers each, there were also two teams of men equipped with shoulder fired Stingers. The real problem was that the unit only had a total of 30 Stinger missiles left and once those were gone the unit's ability to fend off air attack would be greatly reduced.

Chapter 43: Final Thoughts

Late in the afternoon the same day that two airplanes had attacked Fort Somewhere, Colonel Erickson sat in Dr. Stone's office in the village clinic, frustrated.

He had been relieved to hear that there were no casualties from the attack and that his men had even been able to shoot down one of the planes. But the colonel always felt like he was in the wrong place. He'd been back at camp when the village had been attacked twice, and now that he was in the village, his unit had been attacked directly back at camp.

Dr. Stone walked into the clinic and came and sat down with him.

"Sorry for the delay Colonel, but I had to do my rounds on the wounded villagers. As you know most of them are choosing to stay in their homes," he said apologetically.

"Of course Doctor," Erickson replied.

Colonel Erickson focused and his voice grew serious, "I'd like to continue the conversation we were having earlier, before the airplanes paid us a visit." He paused a moment, "How long have you known that we were hit by a nuke and that is what brought us here?"

The doctor's reply sounded like a deflection, "Colonel, I can't even say now that I *know* we were the target of a nuclear weapon, there is no way we could ever really know that for sure."

"Once the Japanese made their presence known, it was just logical to conclude that to be the case. I reasoned that a source of immense energy would have been required, but I didn't suspect the source until now."

Erickson nodded. The doctor's explanation was plausible, but he sensed something was being held back.

231

"What about the elaborate camouflage? Why are they going to the trouble of masquerading their vehicles as mythical monsters?" the colonel asked in a more relaxed tone.

Damon Stone's face drew into a smile with the question, "Ah, I think it's for intimidation purposes. The machinery would seem monstrous to the local indigenous peoples from this time, and in order to control these populations effectively, the Japanese would want to perpetuate this idea. If a tank is merely a tool of men then it won't be feared in the same way as a dragon, which can put fear into the heart of a man. The Japanese have technology, but they'll never have anything close to superior numbers."

Again the colonel nodded his approval. He had already made the same conclusion himself, but wanted to test the doctor.

"So the question is, what do we do now? The presence of the Japanese completely changes our situation," he said.

"Yes indeed," the doctor answered. "I've only given it brief thought, but my suggestion is that we make contact with someone in their leadership and discuss how we could be of mutual benefit to one another."

Erickson raised his eyebrows at this, "Really? So make peace with them."

"Yes sir, I think that makes the most sense. Yes there have been causalities on both sides, but both sides were acting defensively without knowledge of the true situation," the doctor reasoned.

"Old allegiances and national rivalries don't mean anything in this world. They are clearly the power in this region, and really the world. I think our best course of action is to join with them," the doctor concluded.

Erickson thought this a reasonable plan of action, but something about it bothered him. He just needed time to think it through. "I agree that we should try and communicate with them and hopefully head off any more hostilities. I'll get us moving toward that goal."

"Colonel, I'd like to be a part of any face to face interaction if we get to that point," the doctor interjected.

"Of course Damon, I had assumed that you would," Erickson reassured.

* * *

Later that day, Dr. Stone arrived on foot back at Camp Nowhere just as the sun was setting. It was about the time of the summer solstice and the doctor was glad for the extended daylight.

It hadn't been easy to excuse himself from the clinic and all the wounded to trek back to camp, but he *had* to get back. He had uncovered something extraordinary but the battle in the village had forced him to drop everything and head there.

He hadn't managed any real sleep since before then and his fatigue was real. *Not a young man anymore*, he thought to himself with a smile. Nevertheless he continued walking on toward the medical supply tent, and the underground bunker hidden within.

The appearance of the Japanese had been unexpected, but only because he hadn't given it enough thought. He had suspected some kind of nuclear power was involved in the time shift even prior to finding evidence of it. But it hadn't occurred to him that the phenomenon would be a constant in the wake of nuclear detonation.

Right away the doctor saw the presence of the Japanese as good news. Now he knew who the dominant power of the time period was and would be for his life and beyond. And that it was in a fairly modern society delighted him. It was just a matter of contacting them and convincing them of his worth.

Colonel Erickson would help some of the doctor's plan, whether he realized it or not. Damon was hopeful that there would be an in person meeting soon, preferably in Japan but that wasn't likely as a first step. He needed to get in touch with someone of importance in order to initiate back door communications.

It was still a possibility that the colonel would make peace with the Japanese forces and even embrace them as partners, but Damon put the odds on that happening at roughly 5 to 1 against. The colonel was too set in his nationalist ways and possessed a moral compass that would never approve of the methods a bold imperial power would be using to expand itself against primitive people. Damon hoped that all of the men and women in the unit would come along and join with him and perhaps create their own sub group within the Japanese sphere of influence. But whether they did or not, he was determined to make the best out of this opportunity and make sure he came out a winner.

The doctor finally arrived at the medical supply tent, greeted his two guards, and went inside. Collecting a flashlight he proceeded down into the bunker. Once there he hung a box lid over the entrance hole, the rest of the opening already blacked out with blankets. Then he lit two gas lanterns revealing the large chamber, with its work benches and lab equipment, that was now mostly devoid of dirt.

But near the back wall there was a large mound of dirt going most of the way to the ceiling on top of which sat a partially excavated metal sphere, or rather the shattered and torn pieces of what Damon judged *used* to be a sphere. At present he thought it looked most like a metal and dirt brain about five feet across.

The work to uncover this find had been delicate. When he had come across the first small jagged piece of metal he had known immediately that it was something significant. This had caused him to slow his pace and direct his work at the top so as not to undermine the discovery. The painstaking excavation had revealed more than 100 pieces of the thin metal casing dispersed globularly. Dr. Stone could imagine it all compressed back into an intact shape that brought to mind pictures of the Trinity device from 1945.

Damon knew that he was looking at a miracle, an *explosion* buried like shards of broken pottery. Only microseconds after the nuclear reaction had gone critical, the moment the outside metal casing had started separating in the explosion, all of it had been copied and hurtled across space and time only to be entombed here.

Amazing... Everything in the vicinity was captured in that fraction of a second and reproduced here with a null velocity, seemingly ex nihilo, and superimposed with the matter already existing in this universe.

Even as he was still in the process of revealing the bomb shell he knew he wouldn't be able to take it with him when he left for Japan. The only way he could imagine being able to move any of the technology out of the bunker was for the Japanese to take possession of the valley and gain him access to it. That would probably only happen if there was a conflict between the two forces, which Stone was hoping wouldn't materialize. In the meantime he would cover up the exterior of the bunker and find a way to make sure no one rediscovered it.

The colonel is getting suspicious, he thought. *I have to stay at least one step ahead of him or he could destroy my plans.*

I need to get on with recruiting, the two guards and the sergeant aren't enough. I need to talk with Lieutenant Norman some more and I need to ensure I have a woman coming along. The young lady in supply would do, have to bring her into my confidence a little more. But only if the Carlisle woman is resistant, getting her to come along would be most agreeable.

Damon knew that obtaining the company of local women wouldn't be difficult. But for him female companionship was much more than an amorous activity. He needed a woman to discuss his ideas with which required, at minimum, a fluent common language and, preferably, a college education.

The colonel... I hope he doesn't think too much about my past dissertation on parallel universes, incredibly I think it was right on the mark. With so much else for him to think about chances are good that he'll never consider the full ramifications of my theory.

Epilogue: Imperial Intent

Prime Minister Kenji sat at his humble desk looking out the large east facing window of his office. In the last rays of sun he observed a ship docking on the high tide in the small channel below. It was a freighter, bringing in iron ore and other resources from the Tōhoku region of Honshū, a routine shipment.

The youthful forty-five year old leaned back and took a long deliberate draw from a slim cigarette. Holding the smoke in his lungs he turned his attention to the map of Korea that dominated one wall of his office. A red flag was pinned to a spot on the map near the northeast coast of the troublesome peninsula. After a few more moments he released the smoke in a silent hiss through clenched teeth.

For several days something unusual had been happening in this area but it had only been raised to him today. A prime minister can't be bothered with every minor insurgency or logistical mishap after all. But it had suddenly become much, much more.

This wasn't a pack of rebels with stolen guns. Those men had grown old and given up or been exterminated decades before. No, this was something else. With a single machinegun any man could kill a hundred hapless warriors, they were cannon fodder and nothing more. But it took much more than luck or an ambush to swat an airplane from the sky with a single rocket as had been described to him.

Aside from that he only needed to look at the items lying on his desk to know that there was something fundamentally different about the newcomers. The machine pistol was exquisitely made. The fit of the parts, the smoothness of the action, even the finish of the metal more painstakingly crafted than any weapon he'd ever seen.

Then there was the uniform taken from the Chinese prisoner. It was sturdy well-made clothing and had an unusual camouflage pattern but was otherwise unremarkable except for the flag emblems attached to each shoulder. Upon first sight he knew that he had seen this design before. He'd had to consult one of the history books created by the First Ones to be certain. It turned out to be almost an exact match, only the number of white stars in the blue field was different.

The First Ones, those who had seen the older more advanced world first hand, had recorded much information about these people. They had been in a great war against old Imperial Japan. It was this nation the First Ones had said the gods had delivered them from, bringing Hiroshima and Nagasaki to this primitive world to assure the dominance and continuation of the Yamato people.

Kenji had heard the story as a child and now helped to perpetuate it because it was good for morale, but had always wondered if it were really true. But now he *knew*! He knew that the former world had really existed. An entire *world* of cities and industries, almost unfathomable.

But why would the gods suddenly bring in these antagonists? Perhaps it had been decided that the Japanese race had been found wanting after all. Another long inhale of smoke.

Or... perhaps this was a new gift, a means of accelerating their domination of this world.

Kenji stood and picked up another of the trophies from his desk. It was a camera, but again more elegantly crafted than any he had seen before. He pushed two buttons in sequence, as he had been shown, and was looking at a previously taken picture of himself presented on a small video screen of such amazing color and detail he couldn't yet comprehend how it had been manufactured.

He turned the camera body over in his hand, examining once again the writing engraved there. Three simple characters.

日本製

(Made in Japan)

THE END

More Information

For information about *Breaching the Parallel* and upcoming titles in *The Future Past* series please see the flowing resources.

On Facebook search: Breaching the Parallel

http://www.mwanderson.net/

Twitter @MWAndersonFans

Made in the USA
Middletown, DE
31 March 2019